H.B. SALLE

LOVE THY ENEMIES

Blood B4 Betrayal

A Novel

Allegiance Publishing

This book is a work of fiction, names characters, places and incidents are products of the author's imagination or are used fictitiously. Any resemblance to actual events or locales or persons, living or dead, is entirely coincidental.

ALLEGIANCE PUBLISHING

P.O. Box 132, Grand Blanc, MI 48480

ISBN-13: 978-0692328781

Allegiance Publishing is a register trademark

Cover designed by: Thebookcoverdesigner.com/Betibup33

Printed in the U.S.A.

ACKNOWLEDGEMENTS

First off I would like to thank my creator, Mrs. Gloria Jean Lemons. You are the definition of unconditional love without you I wouldn't have the strength to lift my heavy eyelids every morning. I love you Mama Jean.

To my sisters: Tosha; I'm proud of the woman you have become despite our environment growing up. Continue to teach our sister how to be a lady. Tiana; every time I talk to you the more I realize you and I are just alike: Crazy as hell! But no matter what you always there when I need you, I got you sis! Taylor and Tamara; time is flying and it's hard to believe you two aren't kids anymore. I love you both and please don't make me go crazy when I get home!

To My Brothers: Rich Blow; you fathered me because our father never fathered you. You the reason I write, you the reason my veins pump loyalty, D.O.H forever, my baby. Free; you my other half no matter what, we been through it all together and no one knows me like you. Not even me! SB forever my baby. Lil Ray; I'm proud of the man you're becoming, keep doing you. DelJuan and Deandre; if you want to impress me do the complete opposite of what I did growing up. Make our mama proud.

Please bear with me because I must shout out a few people:

Lard (I love you boy!), G.I. (Vernon Turman), Lo-Lo (Don't be mad!), Figgaz (3 cities!), Duice (Am I my brother's keeper?), Supreme, Cipe, Nique (Aye I still love pooh!), Blaze, P.A. 154, MOJO, B.C. GOTTI, Big Brown-El, Johnson-El, B.C. Moe (One Time!), Bayru Duke, Cash, Soulja, Mike Mike, A-Town, Moe Scheme, Champ, Rell, Abdul, Curt-Curt, and all my DAMU's!

Of course I have to mention the big homie, FAMO. You the realist dude from Pontiac without a doubt! Can't wait to read your novel, plenty love and respect!

And most importantly where would I be without the beautiful, Necole Tate. I would've never made it this far without you, and for that I'm forever indebted. Thank you.

I dedicate this book to Anthony Irby, JR, Steven Thomas, Derrick "Coutie" Dudley, Shawn "Nu-Nu" Rutherford, and everyone else I lost through the years.

The cost of living is going up and the chance of living is going down. – Flip Wilson

LOVE THY ENEMIES

Blood B4 Betrayal

Chapter One

Gino

This is most definitely my reality, but I still can't believe this day is finally here. After five long years trapped behind Michigan Department of Corrections walls, I'm at last being released to society. And just like everybody that gets out of Prison says, "I'm not coming back!" I couldn't let that statement escape my lips. I knew I was going back to a life of crime, unlike some niggaz in denial. You can never predict the outcome living that lifestyle.

But I did know one thing for sure and two things for certain, I wasn't going back to the stick-up game. I just did a five year bid for armed robbery and only got one thousand dollars out the deal. That shit didn't add up to me at all! Five years of my life wasted and I regretted committing the crime every time I'd opened my eyes and realized I was dead to the earth. I know I made a dumb move, but you live and you learn.

That was when I was 18 years old, now I'm 23 years old with a more mature state of mind. Not that age has anything to do with maturity, because I believe that maturity has to do with what types of experiences you've had and what you've learned from them. And less to do with how many birthdays has passed. Caught up in my own thoughts, I glanced at my two closest duds in the joint and I couldn't help but smile.

"Aye Gino, what the fuck is you smiling at Lil Homie?" Asked Sandman with a smile on his face as he waited for my answer.

"I'm smiling at yo George Clinton looking ass!" I responded making all of us laugh loud enough to irritate the inmates who didn't find shit funny early in the A.M.

"But on the real, I was thinking about what I'm go do when I touch them streets", I said with a hint of seriousness.

"Stay out there blood and be glad you got a chance to get out this bitch because I ain't ever going home", said Sandman with pure sincerity in his voice and eyes.

Sandman was a real solid dude who caught a life sentence for killing some lame who killed his little brother. I hate to see real niggaz trapped in this Prison system until there last breath. And every time I hear Sandman say he's never going home, my heart cry for a precious life wasted in an artificial world. And although I never told him, I

2

vowed to hold my man down until my casket dropped. I will do this time with him like a nigga suppose to!

"Yeah that's real shit bro, stay out there! I'll be out there with you in a couple more years fam! We go ball out for real!" Said Jay, as he gave my hand a firm handshake.

Jay was a couple years younger than me, and was in the joint for drug possession, his third offense. He was no nonsense, quick to go to war type of nigga. Most of the time me or Sandman had to calm him down from fucking somebody up, but I would've blew my parole in a split second for him; even though he was from Grand Rapids and me and Sandman was from Detroit. He was a loyal ass nigga and I respected that.

"Don't trip I'll be out there just make sure you make it out there, I replied with authority.

"Cell 212 Top, inmate Irby please get your property and report to the officer's station", A.C.O announced over the unit intercom.

"It's that time my peeps." I said as I stood up after hearing my last name being called over the intercom.

Jay and Sandman stood up with an expression on their faces that said they were happy I was getting out, but was sad because a piece of them was leaving. And I felt the same way. I gave my two loyal comrades a hug and fought back a single tear, knowing Sandman and I will never live in the same world again.

"Y'all keep y'all head up to the sky, I love y'all fam. Jay, lay back and come home. Sandman…" I paused to finally let that tear stream down my face and drop on my state-blue shirt. Although Sandman wanted to cry too, life wouldn't let him. He cried enough.

"Make sure you get at me FAM and I'm go shoot some dough your way ASAP. Stay solid my baby and don't let these bitches break you. Y'all got my brother cell phone number so hit me up later this week. One hunnit my baby," and with that said, I walked out of the dayroom wishing I could take my homies with me.

I retreated back to my cell to get my legal work, the only property I was taking with me, and headed to the officer's station. On my way there I said peace to a couple fellas I associated with and kept it moving. When I got to the officer's station C.O. Leslie was standing at the desk. I use to flirt with her even though she was a semi-cute, fat white chick. But hey, a bitch looks is the least of an inmate worries! Inmates pursued female C.O.'s for two reasons: To fuck them or to talk them into bringing in drugs. If you got a chance to fuck a female guard then you knew your game was tight. But if the female guard would bring you in drugs then you controlled the prison and money came nonstop. I didn't have a chance to do either, but I tried hard.

"Mr. Giovanni Irby, I hope you do the right thing and not come back", said C.O. Leslie with compassion in her voice. But her eyes said something totally different. Her eyes said I'll see you again.

"The only way I'll come back is if they turn this bitch into a cemetery", I said calmly. And I meant every word.

Chapter Two

Gino

A fter going through the process of being released, I was given a check for the money I had in my account, and my Greyhound bus ticket to Detroit. A transporter drove me to the nearby bus station, wished me luck, and left me by myself. I took a deep breath and inhaled the fresh air on the cool April morning. I was dressed in a new khaki outfit given to me by M.D.O.C, and I couldn't wait to put it in the trash. I didn't want anything that belong to or reminded me of prison. It was twenty minutes away from 10:00 a.m. which was the time my bus was supposed to arrive.

I looked around in amazement at nothing in particular; I was just enjoying my freedom. In the process of me loving life, the bus finally pulled up. I boarded the bus, handed the driver my tick and sat in the seat next to the window. The whole three hour ride to Detroit I was observing my surrounding and noticing every little thing the average person would never notice. We arrived at the bus terminal in my hometown I haven't seen in years and finally, I believed I wasn't dreaming.

I got off the bus and stretched my arms for a few seconds. I noticed a couple of females sneaking looks at me, speaking amongst themselves and giggling. I looked directly at them with a smirk on my face that revealed my desire to want to fuck them. One of the females bit her bottom lip in lust, while the other one winked seductively. I was 6'2, 190 pounds of pure muscle. If I would've lifted my shirt and showed them my six pack, they would have cum on themselves. I nodded my head at the two women and went about my business. I looked around searching for my little brother who promised to pick me up on time. I looked for a minute and I didn't see him so I walked towards the pay phones. Just as I picked up the phone to dial, somebody tapped me on the shoulder.

"When you done making your call we can leave my baby."

I turned around it was my younger and only brother, Ace.

"My muthafucking baby, what's good my baby!" I gave him a brotherly hug and happiness was written all over his face.

Ace was now 21 years old, and was getting major paper. While I was in the joint he made a come up selling cocaine and heroin aka blow that white girl. He robbed a big time dope man on the west side name Birdie, for a brick of cocaine and twenty- thousand in cash two years ago and hasn't looked back since. It was a stick-up kid ultimate lick and he pulled it off without having to shed blood. After flipping coke for a while he decided to slang blow too, so I introduced him to my connect Mook, while I was in prison. So once the blow business was afloat like the coke was, he hired a couple of workers, sat back and let his money stack. He didn't fuck with too many catz because I always taught him that money breed envy. We never got a chance to discuss his whole operation being that our conversations were always monitored, except on visits. But I was sure he was moving plenty bricks now because he took care of the family. He bought our moms a house and a car, and bought our little sister a car also. He kept my account in prison loaded so I didn't want for nothing my last two years. He even looked out for my girl whenever I asked him to, and that meant a lot to me. I took a step back and looked at him and realized he was a grown man now. He was laid-back and he had the maturity of a forty year old man. I guess money will make you grow up faster than you want too. As always he was fresh to death with a style similar to the rapper Fabulous. He had on some new Jordan's, a crispy pair of Girbauds, a V-neck T- shirt, a Brietling watch and a New Era Detroit Tigers fitted cap. Not to flashy, but expensive was his motto. He looked me up and down and shook his head.

"You gotta come up outta those clothes my dude; you look like you committed a crime!" He said while laughing.

"Yeah I know man, let's get the fuck out of here", I said while seeing if people were staring at me.

I followed him out to his 2004 Mercedes Benz S-Class, silver with stock wheels, we both got in and he pulled off nonchalant.

"DAMN…I ain't know this bitch was plush like this! I know you getting all kinds of pussy driving this bitch! What this hit for?"

"About Eighty stacks, nothing major", he said just as humble.

"Eighty stacks huh? You getting it like that boi."

"Yeah, I'm doing a little something, but we don't have to discuss that now", then he looked at me and put his index finger on his lips.

"Right now all we gone discuss is getting yo ass outta them clothes! We about to hit up Sunset Mall real quick, then we go head to the crib", he turned the music up and let that new Jada kiss song paint us a visual.

We pulled up to the Sunset Mall and parked near an emergency exit a couple feet away from the side entrance. We got out of the car and security pulled up next to us and lowered their window. Ace handed the security guard some money and pulled off smoothly.

"You gotta pay to get V.I.P treatment everywhere you go", said Ace, and then we headed into the mall.

The sight of all the designer stores, jewelry stores, and women brought back a lot of memories and ignited a fire within my heart that had been dark for the past five years. The whole atmosphere was all too familiar, and it was time to get reacquainted with my fashion sense. I looked over at Ace and he smiled at me as if he knew exactly what was running through my mind. Ace then reached in his pocket and pulled out a roll of money the size of a baseball and handed it to me.

"How much is this?" I asked while inspecting the roll of money.

"I think that's only like fourteen-thousand. I would've had more for you but I haven't had a chance to hit the stash house up. So if it ain't enough to get everything you need we'll come back tomorrow.

"Bruh this should be more than enough! Good looking out lil bro."

"Don't even trip, we blood, you ain't got to thank me for shit, this our money! What's mine is yours because you were blessing me before you went to the can. You showed me you ain't care about money and I always live by that code. Never love nothing that…"

"…don't love you back. I can't believe you still remember that shit lil bro! I'm glad you learned something from me."

"I learned a lot from you Gino. You the reason I'm-excuse me-we're here. You taught me everything I know. But we don't have time to be all emotional and shit, we thugs my baby!" We both laughed and gave each

"Yeah you right, it's time to ball out! But let's go get me a phone first just in case I pull a few bad bitches."

We walked inside a Nextel phone store and I purchased the newest phone they had. After leaving there we went into almost every urban store: D.E.M.O, Man Alive, Against All Odds, Jimmy Jazz, and Underground Station, so on and so on. I walked inside of Lids had store and bought twenty fitted hats, all with the old English D on them. We went inside of Footlocker and I spent close to three-thousand dollars in gym shoes alone.

As we were walking out of Footlocker shoe store I noticed a pecan-brown complexion chick checking me out from a distance, I still had on the tan khaki outfit, but all the shopping bags me and Ace had, you wouldn't even notice my attire. I looked cutie in her eyes, penetrating her pupils until she was forced to smile. I smiled back and nodded my head in a way that said 'Come here'. She shook her head no, and nodded the same way I did, gesturing me to come to her. Ace was on his phone talking to some chick in a hushed tone. I walked away from him and approached the cutie with a Casanova expression on my face.

As I got closer I realized she was more attractive than I had thought! She had flawless skin, a petite body with a perfect bubble ass, hazel eyes, perfect teeth, with a 'Halle Berry' short hairstyle to compliment her sharp features.

"Are you going to say something?" She said with a slight smirk on her face.

I didn't even know I was standing there staring at her. You could just stare at her until you got sleepy, that's how captivating her beauty was.

"Huh…damn my bad baby girl. I was too caught up in your appearance. You looking real edible right now and I thought I should let you know that. What's up, my name is Gino. And yours is?" I extended my hand to her after dropping my bags.

"My name is Nadia thanks for the compliment. Is there anything else you want to say to me?" Nadia asked, as she stuck her neck out a little waiting on my response.

I didn't understand her question so I looked at her like she was dumb. Is this bitch waiting on some more compliments? Apology? What?

"Can I get your number so we can spend time together?" I said hoping it was the answer to her question.

"So you really don't remember me, huh, Giovanni Irby?"

I lifted my eyebrows in confusion and tilted my head to the side. This bitch knew my government name, is she the feds! I remember every bitch I fucked, well almost every bitch. But I was certain I didn't fuck this chick.

"You know me? Alright look, if I done robbed your man or something like that, it was about five years ago so fuck that lame, get it in blood," I said, meaning every single word.

She just started laughing out loud as if I said the joke of the century. I got agitated and cut straight to the chase.

"Aye, check this out. You are making me paranoid right now with this guessing game. If you got something to say or if you know something I don't holla at me."

"Your memory is all messed up boy! I'm Nadia Lo-Lo cousin."

"Lo-Lo? Lo-Lo...the only Lo-Lo I know is from Ypsilanti and-oh shit!" It finally came to me, this was my man's Lo-Lo little cousin! Goddamn she grew up to be a bad bitch.

Last time I was down in Ypsilanti was a few months before I got knocked. I was 18 years old and Nadia wasn't shit but 14 years old. She had a major crush on me at the time, but I told her she was too young for me. But that didn't stop her from flirting every time I came around. I reached out and gave Nadia a very affectionate hug, holding her tight and close.

"Damn girl, you look so different I didn't even recognize you! You grew up to be a beautiful woman."

"You just saying that because I'm old enough now and you want some of this pussy!" We both laughed and she couldn't be more real than that.

"What you doing in Detroit, and where my boy Lo-Lo at?"

"I stay in Detroit now. I'm attending Wayne State University and I got my own apartment on the Westside. Lo-Lo still in Ypsilanti. He getting a little money now so he doesn't know how to act. I just talked to him the other day and he supposed to be coming down to Detroit to take care of some business. When did you get out of prison?" She asked, putting her hands on her hips.

"I just got out this morning. Why Lo-Lo soft ass ain't pop at a nigga? He knew how to get in contact with my peoples," I said, clearly displaying anger.

"I don't know you should call him and ask him. I wanted to write you but I knew you wouldn't't've written back because of my age at the time. But then I got caught up in school so much that I blocked everything else out. But you always crossed my mind, you were my first real crush," she said in a low voice as if I had let her down.

"We can't dwell on the past Nadia only focus on the future. How about we exchange numbers, so we can get together one of these days, alright?"

We exchanged numbers quickly and I made sure I stored her number because I couldn't wait to spend time with the young stallion.

"You want Lo-Lo number too?"

"Nawl, just tell him I said what up and give him mine if he ask for it. What you getting ready to do right now?" I asked, looking over at Ace and he was still deep into his conversation.

"I had to pick up a couple things, now I'm on my way home to study for this test I have tomorrow. What are you about to do? It's your first day out, I know you about to get you some pussy! How many bitches you got lined up to fuck?"

"Come on now, cut it out Nadia! I'm about to spend time with my family, a female ain't on my mind at this moment. But I can go fuck who I want because I ain't tied down. I'm single and ready to mingle, you feel me?" I said, hoping she got the hint.

"Yeah whatever! You can't wait to stick that dry dick into something tight, hot and wet so you can stop lying 'Mr. Single and ready to mingle'. You ain't go be single for long, somebody go lock your sexy ass down in a hot second," said Nadia, with a seductive look in her eyes.

"Whoever that somebody is I pray that it's your identical twin. Anybody else, I would be settling for less, you catch my drift?"

"Yes I do. It's time for me to go now. I'm glad we ran into each other, I believe it was fate if you catch my drift. Make sure you call me too, don't be on no B.S…"

"I wouldn't let a miracle pass me if I can reach out and grab it. You just make sure you answer the phone when I call or we go be beefing! Understood?" I replied, putting my hands around her waist breathing in the air that she was breathing out.

15

"Yes I understand, Casanova! You swear you got game. But I'm go let you get back to shopping, call me."

With that being said, we hugged and went our separate ways. Me and Ace went into a couple more stores and went back out to the car. We put most of the bags into the trunk, and the ones that couldn't fit we stuffed them into the backseat of the car. I spent the majority of the fourteen grand and only had twenty-three hundred left. I tried to pass it to Ace while he was on the phone but he shook his head no and looked at me like I disrespected him. He finished his phone conversation up before he started the car and pulled off.

"You got everything you want bro?" asked Ace.

"Yeah, I just got tired. I'm ready to take a shower, eat and dive into some pussy."

"Yeah I feel you my baby. We about to slide to the crib so you can take a shower and get dressed. Then we going to mama house, she is cooking for you as we speak. But speaking of pussy, who was that little chick you was talking too? She was nice, real nice."

"That was Nadia, Lo-lo lil cousin from Ypsilanti. She had a crush on me before I got locked up but she was too young for a real nigga," I answered as I was thinking about how I was going to punish that pussy when I get the chance.

"Shit, she ain't little no more! That's go be the first piece of ass you gone hit."

"Fuck nawl! You already know who getting this dick first."

"Who that slut Zaria? I know you ain't fucking her first."

I looked at my brother as if he was suicidal. "You better watch your mouth little bro before I put these paws on you." We both started laughing together hysterically. He always does that to hear me snap.

"You know I'm just fucking with you bro. I bet you would kill a muthafucka over Zaria, wouldn't you? You need to stop caking like that bro."

"Whenever you fall in love lil bro, then you'll understand. Until then enjoy being a young bachelor. Speaking of Zaria, I gotta call her up.

Chapter Three

Gino

WE arrived at Ace three bedroom house located in Chesterfield Township on 23 mile road and Gratiot, and I never imagined us living in a suburban neighborhood. We repped the hood and loved it so much, we never thought about moving out of it. I guess that's the thoughts that are programmed in our young minds because all we knew was the hood. I for one have never been anywhere outside of Michigan. He parked the Benz in his two car garage right next to his 2003 Range Rover Sport, all black on black, with the black 24 inch Asanti's. We got out the car and gathered all of the bags before going inside the house through the entrance inside the garage. Ace bought the house and was the only one who occupied it while I was locked up. But the house was well furnished and also spotless as if a woman lived with him. From my understanding, no one knew where he lived except our mama, and our little sister Autumn.

"Home sweet home; this is our domain, bro. I paid two- hundred thousand in cash to live like this. It was a minor setback but I bounced back like a rubber band. Come on upstairs so I can show you your room."

He led the way up the stairs and into a nice sized bedroom. The room was plush as if it was on Art Van showroom floor. It had a brand new marble bedroom set, a 60 inch Sony Plasma flat screen that hung on the wall, and different types of electronics I couldn't even recognize. We sat the bags on my bed and Ace pointed to the door across the room.

"That's your bathroom right their Gino. We don't have to argue or fight over who pissed on the toilet no more! Joked Ace.

"Yeah, with your nasty ass! And you had the nerve to tell mama it was me knowing damn well it was you all the time!" I said, thinking back on our childhood.

"You did do it sometimes, but for the most part I was pissing everywhere besides inside the toilet!"

"Them were the good old' days' right there. But you got us outta the slums and I'm proud of you for that, baby boy."

Ace looked at his watch, and clapped his hands together; reminding me we were on a schedule. "We gotta hurry up before mama start calling and going off on us. I got a bottle of Moet Rose you can sip before we leave. I'm about to take a quick shower too, so meet me down stairs when you finished," Ace left and closed the door behind him.

I went into the bathroom and ran the hot water before I finally got into the shower. After taking a shower I went back in the bedroom and begin to rummage through the shopping bags, trying to decide what I wanted

19

to wear. I ended up putting on a pair of smoke grey Roca wear jeans, a white V-neck T-shirt, a pair of all white low-top Air Force 1's and a smoke grey fitted hat with the white old English D. After spraying myself with some Lacoste cologne, and brushing my 360 waves, I was ready to go. When I got downstairs, Ace was in the kitchen sitting at the Island texting on his phone with a bottle of champagne still unopened. He saw me enter the room and passed me the bottle.

"Here, you are drinking this by yourself. This is your day to live like a king my nigga. I see you still got taste in gear, but you missing something," said Ace, looking me up and down.

Ace got up and dashed back up the stairs, and came back a minute later with some grey and white marble Cartier glasses, a diamond encrusted Cartier watch and a 30 carat princess cut diamond chain. I put all the jewelry. And glassed on and then looked in the mirror in the living room.

"That's you big bro. It looks better on you anyway. Now let's get the fuck outta here, grab yo bottle we up."

I grabbed the champagne, popped it open, and begin to drink it straight from the bottle. He decided to drive the Range Rover, so I got in the passenger seat and laid the seat back a little and got comfortable as we headed to mama crib. I decided to call my wifey Zaria to make sure it was going down tonight and just as I expected she was screaming with

20

excitement that I was finally free. I told her to meet me at my mama house so we could eat, chill, and then go back to her place. She agreed, and then we ended our call with a few smooches.

***

Once Ace stacked up enough money he moved our mama out of Detroit to a four bedroom, two bathroom house out in Shelby Township on Springhill Dr., which he paid two hundred-sixty-four thousand in cash for. Mama was driving a 2004 Cadillac SRX, and could get anything she desired from Ace. Money wasn't unfamiliar in our lives anymore, but she still decided to keep her custodial maintenance supervisor job at a company she had been working for, for the past 17 years. Ace and I tried to talk her into retiring early, but to no avail, she wouldn't listen.

Sheryl Jean Jones was now 43 years old and had lived a hard life 39 of those years. She dropped out of High School when she was only 14 years old to take care of her mother who was diagnosed with breast cancer. After a long 7 month battle, she died peacefully in my mama arms. My mama ended up living with her aunt Margie and decided to get a job as a housekeeper to help out with the bills. Instead of going back to school. After years of working she met a nice gentleman by the name of Gerald Giovanni Irby, who worked at a Chrysler Plant. After a year of dating he was murdered in a robbery that went wrong. A young stick-up kid pulled a gun out on him and demanded him to hand over all of his money, but he refused. He had just cashed his paycheck and had planned on buying my mama something nice, so his pride was too strong to bow down to a young punk. The stick-up kid shot him twice in the stomach and fled the scene not even bothering taking the money. My mama was beyond devastated. Not only did she lose the love of her life, a week after his death she found out she was pregnant with me.

A couple years after I was born she met and married a man name Anthony "Ace" Jones. She found herself pregnant yet again with another boy on the way, Ace Jr. A year later we welcomed a girl to the family, Autumn Essence Jones. Autumn was my heart and I protected her, as well as Ace at all cost. My mama relationship with Big Ace was like a rollercoaster. One day they were lovey-dovey, the next day they were fighting like enemies. But it always ended with Big Ace hitting her, and making her cry. And whenever she was in pain, I felt it. Whenever she cried, I cried with her. I sat by my bedroom door protecting my brother and sister from harm's way, and silently cried.

I soon learned what the word hate felt like because I hated Big Ace, I wouldn't call him daddy. He told me to call him daddy all the time, but I wouldn't listen to him. Many nights I thought about killing him while he was asleep. I had a red suite my mama bought me from the Salvation Army that I couldn't wait to wear. I fantasied about wearing it to Big Ace funeral one day. I would fantasize about taking a kitchen knife and stabbing him continously times until he stops breathing. Then one day my fantasy came into fruition.

I was 10 years old and fed up with the crying. I made a vow to myself that this would be the last day he put his hands on my mama. At around 1:00 a.m., I snuck out of my room and crept to the kitchen. I walked past Big Ace who was snoring peacefully on the couch as if he was an angel at heart. I went into the kitchen and grabbed a knife out of the dish rack. I crept back into the living room and stood over him, watching his stomach rising up and down. I held the knife above my head and brought it down as hard as a 10 year old could, and it slid straight through his stomach. Blood squirted on my face and Big Ace screamed instantly in agonizing pain which made me flinch. I took a few steps back, and smiled at my work of art.

I heard my mama getting up so I ran back to my bedroom and hid under the blanket on my bed. Big Ace started cursing and continuously screaming while my mama tried her hardest to help him. She tried to call an ambulance but he told her not to, something about he had warrants. He did some more cursing and then told her to take him to the hospital before he bled to death. When they left together I waited five minutes before climbing out of my bed to check on Ace and Autumn, and they were still sound asleep. I slowly walked into the living room and blood was everywhere! I smiled at the thought of finally wearing my red suit. After staring at the blood for a while, I went into the kitchen and grabbed a pint of ice cream out of the freezer, sat at the kitchen table and finally ate in peace. My mama arrived back at home a few hours later without Big Ace. And that was the last time any of us seen him.

I snapped out of my day dreaming session when Ace pulled up to my mama house. I finished off the little champagne I had left even though I didn't even remember drinking it.

"You straight bro? You over there quiet and shit," asked Ace.

"Yeah, I'm good, just happy to be out bruh."

We both climbed out the truck and the beaming sun was still shinning bright. My buzz started to kick in and I felt euphoria! I discarded the empty bottle in the trash can in the front of the house and put my phone in my pocket. My mama and Autumn must have heard us pull up, because they were walking out the house followed by a few of my uncles, aunts and cousins.

"Hey baby! Gimme some love boy, welcome home," greeted my mama, smiling from ear to ear. She still looked young as ever and kept her body in shape. She was one of the women who genetics blessed her to age gracefully.

"What's up mama? How old are you now 21?" Everybody laughed

"Come here Autumn, you acting like you don't miss yo big bro!"

"Boy, you know I missed your crazy self!" I hugged my little sister who was now a grown woman.

24

She was now 20 years old, attending Baker College on a paid scholarship. She was always smart but dumb when it came to choosing the right boyfriend. Ace had to pistol-whip her last boyfriend two months ago for calling her a bitch. He a better man than me because I probably would've murked his ass. The rest of my family members came up hugging me, telling me how much they miss me but never sent me a dime, let alone wrote a one sentence letter. I pretended that I really cared about the artificial love that they were giving me, and in turn gave them all artificial smiles and hugs. Ace looked at me and smirked because he knew I didn't fuck with our family like that. They were fake and I couldn't stand it.

We all walked in the house and mama gave me a quick tour elaborating on her decorations. She was talking a hundred miles an hour, but I really wasn't listening, the champagne had me zoning out. I was just happy that she was happy.

On top of that I was hungry as fuck! We had fried chicken, macaroni and cheese, sweet potatoes, collard greens, golden buttery biscuits, corn on the cob, and for dessert, my all-time favorite banana pudding and vanilla ice cream. I ate like I never ate before and my mama was enjoying the sight, her baby was home.

"Old lady, you still know how to put your foot in some soul food-wait a minute, what's this, is this a toe nail!" I joked as I pretended I was pulling something out of my mouth, causing everybody to laugh.

I wiped my mouth with a napkin and took a sip of the homemade lemonade just as my phone began to ring.

"Who this?" I answered

"Who this? That's not how you answer the phone when your wife calls you?" Said Zaria half-jokingly.

"What's good baby, that's my bad I didn't look at my caller I.D. Where you at?" I asked

"I had to run to my grandma's house to take her some money. I'm going to be pulling up at your mother's house in a few minutes baby."

"You missed dinner we just got done eating. Do you want me to make you a plate to go?"

"As much as I love your mother's cooking, I have to pass. The only thing I want to eat tonight is you," responded Zaria, with a slight purr to her voice.

"I wish I could respond to that, but my mama sitting right next to me," I looked at my mama and she rolled her eyes at me.

"But…," I continued, "I will respond to that whenever we get to where we going, you feel me?" I could hear her giggling on the other end.

"You bet not have me on speakerphone, Gino!"

"Now why would I do that?"

"I don't know I was just making sure. I don't want your mother to think I'm a freak."

"Oh she already knows that!" We both laughed outrageously.

"Boy shut up! You so silly, I'm pulling up right now, come open the door."

I hung up the phone and went to the bathroom to quickly wash my hands and rinse my mouth out with Listerine. When I got to the front door Zaria was just climbing out of her 2004 Jeep Liberty. Damn, I missed the fuck outta my baby!

Zaria Valencia Robinson was without a doubt the one I would walk down the aisle with in the near future. We've known each other for as long as I can remember. Zaria would always come to our house whenever her mother decided to visit my mama, which was almost every day. One day while our mothers were out clubbing, I hit Zaria with the coldest game an 8 year old could come up with. I hit her with the classic game that was passed down to me from one of my classmates. I wrote her a note that said: Do you like me? Yes, No, or maybe circle one. Needless to say, she chose yes and that's the day we became an official couple. We could never get enough of each other's presence. We were an item for 6 years straight and broke up our first year of High School because I wanted a variety of pussy. She found out I was seeing another chick on the side and we broke up. She stayed mad at me for a couple of months then we were back cool. It's like we became closer when we were just best friends, we talked more to each other every day.

I was a freelancer when it came to girls, and she ended up hooking up with a square ass mofo name Darius. I was beyond jealous now that she was seeing another nigga. I tried to make her cheat on that bum with me but she was too loyal and faithful. Although I didn't like her new boyfriend, we were still close. And we were still deeply in love which is why she blamed me for the separation every time we held a conversation. A year into their relationship her boyfriend did the unthinkable… He cheated. She called me crying her eyes out, and once again blaming me for her turmoil. I was hurt and furious. Furious that he broke her heart, and hurt that I let him break her heart.

They ended up breaking up after I whuppped Darius ass up and down 7 mile. A few months later on her 16th birthday, I told her I wanted to be with her forever. We became a couple again and haven't looked backed since. Even when I was sentenced to those five years flat, she stayed by my side the whole time. And I couldn't ask for a more loyal down chick. Sure I fucked other bitches on the low, but they can't compare to my baby. And once I get married I'm done with the player life.

Zaria walked up to the porch and gave me a hug that spoke for itself. I leaned down and kissed her passionately on her soft, luscious lips then stuck my tongue in her mouth letting it entwine with hers. I ended the kiss and looked into her eyes with an apologetic expression on my face.

28

She was looking sexy as ever her skin complexion was brown as caramel, she had nice C-cup perky breast, her eyes were slanted like she had Chinese in her bloodline, but he hips and fat ass complemented the package. She was now 22 years old, but her birthday was only a few weeks away.

"I missed you so much, Gino! Promise me you'll never leave me again," she demanded as her eyes begin to tear up.

I knew it was impossible to promise such a thing I had no control over, but I still found myself saying…

"I promise."

She smiled and gave me a quick kiss, and then we went in the house with some type of contentment. Zaria spoke to my family and gave my mama and Autumn a hug. My mama loved Zaria as if she was her own child and she knew how much I loved her too. I told everybody I was leaving and gave everybody a hug, even the fake family members.

"Aye bro, let me holla at you before you slide off," said Ace.

We walked outside to the side of the house where no one could see or hear us. Ace pulled out a chrome 45 forty-five Taurus pistol and held it out towards me.

"What the fuck you doing bro? You know I just got out!" I asked taking a couple steps back from him.

"I know bro; I can't let you be out here without a banger. These goons ten times grimier than they were when you went it. Niggaz ain't got any respect or morals, anybody can get it now. I can't have you out here naked. As long as you follow the law, you ain't got to worry about shit. So here, take it," He held the gun out again for me to grab it.

I thought about it for a brief second and he was on point as usual. I took the pistol and shoved it on my waist line after I checked the chamber.

"You right lil bro, good looking. What we got up for tomorrow?" I asked, as I looked around to make sure no one was watching.

"I'm picking you up at eight in the morning so make sure you are ready. We gone talk business and the role you're going to be playing. Then we are going car shopping after we leave the Secretary of State so you can get your licensed. Right now go get you some pussy and I plan on doing the same thing."

"Aight, I'll be ready in the morning so don't be late. Love is love."

"Love is love, my baby."

I went back in the house to give my mama and sister a kiss, and said my final farewells. Me and Zaria jumped in her jeep and pulled off into the clear night.

Chapter Four

Gino

Thirty minutes later we pulled up to Zaria's two bedroom house on Hartwell right off Puritan and Schaffer. The block was a fairly a nice one, you could tell that good people stayed in the neighborhood by the maintenance of their property. She pulled the Jeep all the way into the backyard and parked right in front of the garage. I grabbed the handle of my 17 shot handgun and climbed out the car cautiously.

"This is a nice house baby, I see you've been living real comfortable," I said while checking out my surrounding. You could never be too careful but the way I was looking around I had to remind myself I wasn't in prison anymore.

"Yeah I guess. I'm ready to move though, I think I want a condo by the river closer to my job," said Zaria as I followed her to the side door.

Zaria opened the door and we were greeted by central air, the smell of fruity lotions, and a black cat lightly meowing. We walked up the few stairs and into the kitchen which was organized and spotless.

"Well, this is where I've been staying for the past 3 years, baby. You want something to drink? "She asked, as she opened the refrigerator door.

31

"Nawl, I'm good. I do need to go take a piss, where the bathroom at?"

"Go through the living room and it's the last door down the hallway, the door should be opened," responded Zaria, as she took a sip of her Hawaiian Punch.

I followed her instructions, but when I got to the bathroom door that was supposed to be open, I thought I heard something coming from the room across from the bathroom. I reached under my shirt and gripped the pistol handle until my knuckles begin to throb. I opened the door with caution and the light was on. The bedroom was turned into a makeshift closet because it was partially empty, only occupied by shoes and clothes that were scattered everywhere.

I slowly walked to the actual closet located at the far end of the room and snatched open the door only to find more shoes and handbags. As I was about to turn and leave I felt a hand touch my left shoulder catching me by complete surprise. I swiftly freed the gun from my waist and turned around in the same motion pointing it in the face of the perpetrator which was my future wife.

"Damn girl, what the fuck are you doing? I could've just shot yo fucking head off! Let your presence be known, don't be sneaking up on me like that!"

I yelled in a stern voice and I replaced the gun back on my hip.

"What the fuck wrong with you, boy! You just had a gun pointed in my face and you have the nerve to act like you mad! Why the fuck you have a gun anyway, you just got out of damn prison!" Zaria yelled, clearly upset and frightened.

"Stop fucking yelling!" I yelled

"You stop fucking yelling!" She yelled back.

I had to take a deep breath and get my thought together and calm the situation down because I was the one to blame. Even though she scared the shit out of me, I shouldn't have let my paranoia get the best of me.

"My fault baby, I was on some paranoid shit. I had thought I heard something in here, I'm sorry baby," I grabbed Zaria, kissed her on the forehead and hugged her tight. Her small body was still shaking.

"You forgive me?" I asked with pure sincerity.

She looked me in the eyes with some type of relief and shook her head yes with adorable pouty lips. I leaned down and kissed her softly, stealing her breath away from her.

"Now let's get upstairs so I can kiss them other lips!" Zaria giggled, and then turned to leave as I smacked her ass.

After Zaria went upstairs to wait on me, I went to finally use the bathroom and proceeded to join my baby for some well-deserved fucking. Zaria already had her skirt off and was in the process of taking

33

off her pants just as I made it too the room. The sight of her perfectly shaped ass swallowing her black silk thong, instantly made my dick hard. I stood there at the threshold and quietly watched, not wanting to ruin the allure of a woman undressing. After completing the task of removing her pants, she slowly turned around and caught me admiring her flawless body that I haven't seen in what seemed like a lifetime.

She seductively walked over to me and kissed me hard enough to lose my balance for a brief moment. I felt her tongue dance with mine; only causing my erection to grow harder to the point it forcefully tried to escape my jeans. She hastily pulled my shirt over my head as I unbuckled my belt, but had to pause for a second once I realized I still had my gun on my waist. I pulled it out and walked over to the nightstand right beside the bed and placed it there. I got back to the task at hand and finally took my pants off as Zaria was rubbing and licking on my stomach. I forced her to stand back up and continued to suck on her tongue as I reached around and squeezed both of her ass cheeks aggressively which made her moan into my mouth.

I laid her down on the king sized bed and began to suck and lick on her neck. She moaned louder while firmly grabbing my dick almost pushing me over the brink. I had to remind myself to concentrate on not nutting although it's been a while since I had a woman touch any part of my body in a sexual manner. I reached behind her back and unlatched her black silk bra, and then pulled the bra completely off exposing her soft and perky breast. Her nipples stood at attention as I planted soft kisses and caressed them in a circular motion. Her breathing start to speed up as my tongue darted at her erect nipples. I worked my way down to her stomach and gave it the same treatment as her breast, grabbing both of her hips as I sucked on her navel.

I pulled off her thong that was saturated with her pussy juices and tossed them to the side. After taking a look at her clean shave pussy, I prayed it was still tighter than a fist. I proceeded to kiss all over her thighs and the inside of her thighs close enough to her fat pussy lips I grazed them with my nose. The scent of Victoria Secret Love Spell lotion was exuding from her coochie. Zaria started to moan even louder and breathing heavier in anticipation of the inevitable. I kissed the inside of her thighs a few more times before spreading her pussy lips with two fingers and gently blowing on her stiff clitoris. As an involuntary action she flinched and then spread her legs wider. I kissed her clit and licked it while inserting my finger into her tight dripping pussy. She began to squirm and scream uncontrollable as her juices started to flow like a waterfall. I enjoyed drinking her sweet fluids while she rotated her pelvic bone, grinding into my face with both hands on top of my head pushing me deeper into her wet box.

I licked and fingered her in unison until her body started to shake rapidly and she came viciously in my mouth. I lifted up and she pulled my face to hers and begins to suck her own juices from my mouth. Zaria then flipped me on my back and gave me the same treatment I gave her. She started kissing on my neck, then down to my chest, then down to my stomach which she gave special attention too. She quickly pulled off my Dolce & Gabana boxers and grabbed my dick with a mean grip. Her kissing and licking the head while still looking me in the eyes was almost unbearable to deal with, so I had to close my eyes. Finally, she put the whole nine inches in her mouth and sucked it like a pro! My toes curled up from the wet and warm sensation on her tongue, and just as I expected I could feel myself start to nut 3 minutes into the blowjob. I couldn't fight it any longer and I lifter her head up, I know she didn't like swallowing but she disregarded my warning and swallowed every last drop!

My dick was tingling with pleasure as it went limp in her hands. Zaria climbed on top of me and turned into the 69 position, her pussy was poked out towards my chin and I wasted no time sucking on it as she begin to bring my dick back to life. I grabbed both of her ass cheeks and let my tongue explore her brown eye. She flinched hard at the touch of my tongue licking her sacred hole, I licked it again and she moaned loud enough for the neighbors to hear. She leaned back and sat on my face, rocking back and forth as I continued to suck her voraciously. She came again in a matter of seconds as she bounced up and down on my face.

My dick was back hard as a rock and she turned around to face me and lowered herself onto it slowly. The intense pleasure made me resent myself for getting locked up making me miss out on one of the most precious gifts given by God to women: A vagina! I grabbed her hips and helped her rotate up and down, round and round. I lifted her up and flipped her on her back and started fucking her missionary style, hammering her wet pussy. She was screaming my name and moaning with no regard of anyone that could possibly hear her. I then flipped her over and started hitting it from the back. Her juices were dripping down her legs and on the bed and the sight of that drove me crazy! I took a couple more pumps and I exploded inside of Zaria, my future wife.

******

I was disturbed out of my sleep by a sharp creak I thought I had heard. I listened carefully, but only heard silence in the darkness. I looked over at the nightstand where my pistol was resting, and the digital clock read 2 a.m. As I was about to dismiss the thought of hearing anything and go back to sleep, I heard another floorboard creak, and a very fait mumble. I reached over and grabbed my gun and checked the chamber slowly, making sure I had one ready to let go. I glanced over at a peacefully sleeping Zaria, and wondered who the fuck would break in my baby house? Was they there thinking she was alone? It really didn't matter because they were there, and shouldn't have been.

I heard another floorboard creak and noticed that whoever it was, was getting even closer. I reached over and shook Zaria's shoulder gently to wake her up; I didn't see how she could not hear the intruders.

"Huh…?" said Zaria, with a dry voice. I put my fingers to her lips signaling her to be quiet.

"Ssh, don't say anything; I just need you to shake your head yes or no when I ask you a question. Do you have a roommate?" I whispered, and of course she shook her head no.

"Does anybody besides you have a key to this house?" she shook her head no again.

Her eyes were wide with confusion at both of my questions, and she probably thought I was crazy.

"Look baby, somebody is in this house, and-," before I could even finish my sentence, we both heard the footsteps slowly climbing the stairs. Zaria had fear written all over her face.

"I need you to climb out of bed quietly and hide on the side of the bed. Zaria, we going to be o.k., just don't move until I tell you too, alright?" She shook her head yes as a tear dropped down her face.

She did as I told her too, and I could still hear the footsteps slowly climbing the stairs. I had the gun still in my hand ready to blast if need be. I got out of the bed as discreetly as I could, and crouched near the door leading downstairs. My heart started to thump rapidly raising my chest, not knowing what awaited me in the next few seconds. I just got out of jail today and I was already in a life or death situation! I wondered if it was more than one of them, and prayed I didn't have to kill one of these niggaz. After listening carefully, I could hear two different footsteps. I was crouched close enough to the door that I could grab the first intruders arm if he opened the door with his gun in his right hand. Sweat begins to gather on my forehead and trickled down my face, I didn't know what the outcome would be but I knew in my heart I had to protect Zaria by risking my own life.

One of the intruders reached the top of the stairs and placed his hand on the doorknob. He waited close to ten seconds and then slowly with his left hand, as I anticipated he would. He pushed the door open far enough for him to peek in, and was unaware of how dark the room would be. He defiantly couldn't see me although I was within his arm reach if he happened to look down. He looked in for a few more seconds and I'm guessing, figured we were still asleep. But he was in for a rude awakening!

The first intruder opened the door wider, and took a step in the room in slow motion. Just as I expected his gun was in his right hand slightly pointed at the floor. When he stepped in enough for me to make my move, I grabbed his right hand, leaped up and hit him in the face with my gun and twisted his wrist at the same time, forcing him to drop his gun! I disarmed him so fast; his partner didn't even see what happened. I held on to the first intruder, reached over his shoulder with my pistol and shot the second intruder who was halfway down the stairs, as a grunt escaped his lips once he landed with a hard blow. The one I was holding onto was trying to wrestle himself free, but he was unsuccessful I then hit him with the butt end of the gun right to his temple. He dropped to the floor unconscious and just as I predicted, his partner that I shot fled the scene leaving his partner in crime to fend for himself, fucking coward.

I could hear Zaria crying she was still hiding on the other side of the bed, probably scared to death. I flicked on the light switch, as I tried to catch my breath and slow down my heart rate. I looked down at the motionless body and his nose was bleeding profusely. I lifted my foot up in the air and stomped him as hard as I could in the stomach. He became conscious once again as he spit up blood, and moaned in agonizing pain. I leaned down over his body and pressed the gun against his forehead.

"Aghhhh! Come on dog, please don't kill me man! I know I fucked up, but don't take me out, B! I got a little girl at home dog, and she-"

"Fuck yo daughter you bitch ass nigga! You should've thought about that before you brought yo monkey ass up in this muthafucka!" I said, cutting the young dummy pleading short. I steadily held the gun up to his forehead, while I looked over in Zaria's direction she was still on the floor unseen.

"Zaria, get up baby, it's cool, you can stand up," I said, in a reassuring tone.

Zaria stood up with her face stain with tears, dressed in nothing but a sheet that covered her naked body. Her eyes became wider when she seen a nigga bleeding under the watchful eye of my chrome forty-five. She gasps, as one of her hands covered her mouth from letting out a loud scream.

"Zaria, I need you to get it together baby, we going to be good. Just listen to me, okay?" I asked as she shook her head yes.

"Alright, the first thing I need you to do is hurry up and get dressed. Then I need you too hand me my phone-"

"Please man don't kill me! I swear I will leave town, you'll-"

"Didn't I say shut yo bitch ass up! You say something else without my permission then I'm putting a bullet in yo head!" I shoved the pistol deeper into his forehead causing him to squeeze his eyes shut in pain.

"Zaria, you listening to me?"

"I'm listening baby. I'm scared!"

"I know baby, but we going to make it through this together. I need you to be strong for me, okay?"

"Okay," she replied as she wiped the tears from her face.

"Good. I need you to put on some clothes then grab my phone and call my brother for me. Can you do that, baby?"

"Yes, I'm about to do it." Said Zaria, as she walked over to her clothes and got dressed.

"Now listen you dumb ass bitch, I'm not about to sit here and play kiddy games with you. If you plan on seeing your daughter again I advise you to comply. The first time I feel like you're not being honest, you will have a closed casket, understood?" I asked taking a look over at Zaria who was fully dressed and calling Ace on my phone.

"Yea-yeah, I understand man. I just wanna live," the young nigga pleaded with tears rolling down his face.

Zaria walked over to me and handed me the phone with a shaking hand. I put the phone up to my ear and still concentrated on the defenseless hostage. The phone rung four times before Ace answered with a groggy voice.

"What's up bro, you know what time it is, Ace asked.

"Listen bro, I gotta major problem on my hands right now. I need you to get over here ASAP, and bring a couple niggaz with you. Hurry the fuck up too bro, I really can't say too much, but I also bodied a nigga," I told Ace without taking a breath.

"What the fuck happen? Matter fact don't go nowhere, I'm on my way right now!" Ace hung up the phone.

"Now back to you, fuck boy. Why are you here, and don't say to steal either. I'm far from stupid playboy."

"Man, on some one hunnit shit, we thought you were Ace."

"You thought I was Ace? So, if I was Ace what did you plan on doing, killing him?" I asked in confusion. Why would he think I was Ace?

"This not my call, man. I was just here to do my job, and that was to kidnap him. He got a hundred grand tag on his head, but they want him alive."

"Who are they?" I asked calmly.

"Man…if I tell you they go kill me and my family," he replied with total fear in his eyes."

I hit him with the pistol again causing a cut to split open above his eyebrow.

"Now you either tell me, or I'm going to punish yo ass until you tell me. Make a choice."

"Alright, alright B! It's the Red Mafiya," he announced as his voice cracked. Even my heart skipped a beat when he revealed who was behind the price tag on my brothers head.

The Red Mafiya was the biggest blood gang in the whole Midwest and east coast. It was founded in Detroit on the eastside by a dude name

Slime. Slime used to belong to Head bangers, another blood gang that was birthed in Detroit in the early 90's. After going to prison and becoming an OG with the Head bangers, he decided to branch off and start his own set with the approval of the top dogs. After getting the necessary blessing from the OG's in California, Slime started the set and took it to a level that was never seen before. Muthafucka's knew they couldn't win if they had a problem with the Red Mafiya, so you either joined them, bow downed or stayed out there way. They ran a multi-million dollar enterprise, several Real Estate and construction companies; they even had their hand in the rap industry. They had high ranking police on their payroll that turned the other cheek whenever necessary. After five police officers were murdered while on duty by some Red Mafiya members, the police decided living was more important than serving the law. And to top everything off, Slime use to be my best friend when we were younger!

I snapped out of my daze, and focused back on the hostage. I shook my head in frustration, what has Ace got us into? Fuck!

"Why would the Red Mayfia want my brother kidnapped?" I asked, praying he had the answers. But more than likely he was just a crash dummy that only was there to collect and knew nothing.

"I swear on my dead sister I don't know why. They never tell us why, I just took the job. They give us enough info to get the job done."

I looked over at Zaria and she was sitting on the edge of the bed looking off into space. I stood up with the gun still pointed at this young nigga, as I took a couple steps back and leaned down to pick up the Glock .40 that I forced him to drop.

"Who was that pussy that came with you?" I asked.

"That was my man's Peanut. Is he dead?"

"Dead? That fuck boy took off and left you stuck! Oh, I popped his bitch ass, he somewhere hiding bleeding to death. I'm mad I missed his fucking head! Aye, baby bring me my pants," she brought me my pants and I managed to put them on and still aim the gun. My phone rung once before I answered it.

"Talk to me, bro."

"I just pulled up and the front door is wide open. I'm on my way in so don't get to shooting."

"Aight, come upstairs. If you brought somebody with you tell them to check the whole house," I told Ace, then hung up.

I heard footsteps downstairs and finally I was relieved to know I had reinforcement. I really took a deep breath once Ace entered the bedroom with a Mac 90 in his hand ready to shoot.

"Look bro, this pussy ass nigga and another nigga broke in the house thinking I was you. The other nigga got away after I shot him, but this nigga said they came to kidnap you. And guess who sent them…" I paused for a second, but before I could tell him he answered my question.

"The Red Mafiya sent them," said Ace, and he said it in a calm matter as if it was no big deal. Did he know they were after him? Why didn't he tell me? Why did they put a tag on his head anyway?

"Don't even trip right now, Gino. I'll explain shit to you later, right now I need you and Zaria to gather whatever y'all can and put it in the Jeep and my truck. No furniture though, I'll replace that myself. Needless to say, but you can't live here anymore. We gone take care of this fuck nigga, just get what y'all can and head to my crib."

Five of Ace's goons came up the stairs, all carrying a weapon that shot fifty or more. Ace pointed to the hostage laying on the floor.

"Y'all get that nigga and take him to the hideout, we bout to make a 'Saw' movie the way we gone torture this nigga!"

The goons snatched him up as he protested and screamed, but that wouldn't help him at all. His fate was already sealed. Ace and I looked each other in the eyes and I knew he was deep in the streets. Deeper than I could ever imagine.

Chapter Five

Gino

I Woke up later that morning at 9 a.m. still in awe at what transpired at Zaria's house. I'm actually supposed to be in the morgue right now, but my intuition served me right. I knew something was wrong the moment we pulled up, I just had a feeling. My state of paranoia saved our lives; I guess you can never be too paranoid. I wonder if I was still asleep and they did kidnap me. How would they deal knowing I wasn't Ace? Probably with a bullet to the head! But why would they think I was even Ace? Were they watching Ace when he dropped Zaria off money for me? How long have they been watching him? Why was the hit out on him anyway? Ace and I have a lot to talk about today; I need to know what's going on.

I sat up in the bed and looked over at Zaria who was still sound asleep, breathing lightly. I slid outta the bed as quietly as I could making sure not to disturb my wifey. I walked to my bathroom to take a piss, brush my teeth, and then washed my face. I had to go back in the room to put some gym shorts on, and then grabbed my gun from under my pillow. I checked the chamber to make sure it was loaded, and headed down stairs. I heard the sound of a T.V. as I walked down stairs, gun in hand. I reached the living room and Ace was watching CNN. He looked away from the T.V. for a split second to see who had entered the room, then diverted his attention back to the news. I sat on the love seat and sat my pistol on the coffee table.

"You good, bro?" asked Ace, without taking his eyes off of the T.V.

"Yeah, I'm kosher. What about you?"

"I'm straight. We took care of that lil misunderstanding from last night, he'll never speak again," retorted Ace, as he lit up an OG Kush blunt. He inhaled a cloud of thick white smoke, and continued to talk.

"That's all my fault bro for not putting you up on game. I just wanted your first day out to be stress free, that's why I didn't mention it. But I'm glad I gave you that burner, if they would've snatched you up, bodies would've been dropping until I got you back," he paused for a second to hit the Kush again, and blew the smoke towards the ceiling.

"That shit was crazy, but I was thinking on my toes. I still wanna know how the fuck did they get in?"

"I have no idea. I'm still tryna figure out why would they come for me at your girl house? They must've spotted me going over there the other day when I took her that money."

"They had to be following you. Why Slime got a hit on you anyway? The last time I checked y'all were still cool, what happened?" I finally asked

48

"We were still cool at that time; well at least until he found out I was the one who robbed birdie. It turns out Slime was the one who fronted Birdie that brick and that was his twenty racks too. So Slime sent some little niggaz to holla at me while I was at the Goodnight Lounge a few weeks ago to come collect, and I told them to suck my dick the long way," said Ace, as he tapped the ashes into the tray sitting beside him.

"So let me get this straight, you rather put your life on the line then pay that little money back, bro? That's some stupid ish-,"

"Fuck nawl! Do I look stupid to you bro? I would've been paid that lil shit I took in a second! Slime sent them lame's to me telling me he want twenty-five grand from me every month for the next 5 years! That clown smelling himself and he got life fucked up! He ain't dealing with any hoe nigga, I don't give a fuck who you are or what you claim! Fuck that pussy nigga bro, if he wants a war then that's what he go get. Numbers don't move me!

Ace was beyond mad and I had a feeling there wasn't no easy solution to this problem. I would've told them bitches to suck my dick too, twenty-five stacks a month? That was some crazy shit to even propose, especially coming from Slime. We've been knowing that nigga since pre-school! We stayed on the same block for 17 years, Wade Street. I mean, we did it all together from fucking hoes to shooting at niggaz. We were together every day, if you see him, you seen me right beside him. But Slime was always deep off into gangbanging and I was never down with that. Eventually we grew apart but we were still cool, we were Wade Boyz. But now he probably thinks Ace fucked him over by robbing one of his workers. I'm pretty sure if Ace knew it was Slime product he would've never took it, but what's done is done, where do we go from here is the million dollar question. Ace put what was left of the blunt in the ashtray and begins to surf through the channels.

"So what's next, what's the plan now?" I asked

"Shit, get money! That's all we can do, but if he send another messenger my way its go be all out war! I'm killing that Clown Slime my damn self, and that's on my life! I might not live to enjoy the money but as long as he dead, I'm content."

"Listen bro; never react off of your feeling when it comes to the game. If you stay humble you'll get the same results. You gotta realize that murder is a thinking man's game, so you need to take your heart up outta it or you won't last long in a sea full of sharks. I'm riding with you right or wrong, you feel me"

"I feel you my baby. I'm just tired of his fake ass throwing his weight around as if he's untouchable. I'm fed up bro…I'm fed up," Ace emphasized while shaking his head.

"I know lil homie, just stay humble. As of now we just go lay low and get this paper. If push comes to shove, I'll call my man's down in Flint, and they'll clean up the streets for a flat fee. When unfamiliar faces start blazing at niggaz, they don't know where it's coming from. I got all kinds of connects while I was in the joint, that shit was like a big ass convicts convention."

"Speaking of connects, yours been fucking me over for the past year," Ace announced.

"Who Mook?"

"Yeah Mook! That bitch ass mark been taxing me all this time for a kilo of blow, but serving other customers regular price. That's cool though, I found another plug with some grade-A shit for the low. I would've shot that fuck boy if it wasn't for you."

"Damn, I know Mook ain't do no hoe shit like that. Don't even trip; I'll holla at that O.G. when I get a chance. He still stays out there in Taylor on Wood creek Drive?"

"Hell Yeah, he still in that same big ass house."

"I'm go sit down and talk to Mook. What you got lined up for me on the business tip? I know you moving heavy weight now living this good," I said looking at Ace.

"Yeah, we moving more work that ever imagined. My man's Mitch on his way back from Houston with twenty bricks of Caine. We got fifteen already at the stash house and three bricks of heroin left but it won't last long. That's why I'm glad you're here because you gone take care of everything dealing with the heroin business. Like I told you I got a new connect I haven't even coped from yet but I did sit down and discussed prices with him. He a solid dude and I want you to holla at him. His name is Profit; let me know when you ready to politic wit him."

"Alright, I'll let you know just gimme a minute. We might not need to switch plugs yet, let me talk to Mook first. We'll talk more about this later, I'm about to hop up in this shower and try to wash off the memories from last night. I'll catch up with you in about an hour," I said, as I stood up to leave.

"Oh yeah, hold up Gino. Grab that bag on the dining room table, that's you right there," said Ace, while pointing to the dining room.

I walked into the room and a black duffel bag was sitting on the table. I unzipped the bag and once I looked inside of it, I felt short winded. Inside the bag were bundles of hundred dollar bills stacked neatly with rubber bands around every stack.

"Bro how much money is this?"

"That ain't shit but like two hundred thousand. That's pocket change you can splurge with. Get whatever you want, just make sure you spend it all, you feel me?" said Ace, and smiled arrogantly.

Chapter Six

Gino

It's been three weeks since the attempted kidnapping incident at Zaria's old house on the west side, and the Red Mafiya didn't try to snatch up Ace again. We were still on high alert because the anticipation was nerve wrecking. When somebody is coming for you but you never know when, you tend to look over your shoulders every second, and everybody is a potential enemy.

I stopped at a Red Light on Gratiot Avenue in my brand new 2004 BMW 760Li, white on white, with the white 24 inch Giovanni's. Ace was tripping when I first bought it; I called my baby cocaine on a napkin. I dropped eighty large on it with that two-hundred grand Ace smashed on me. I leased a condo off the riverfront where I and Zaria now reside. Not to mention Zaria birthday just passed so I bought her a 2004 BMW M3, white on white, just like daddy Beemer. I only paid sixty grand for her shit, but she deserved it and much more.

Right now I was on my way to Nadia's apartment on 7 mile by Greenfield. Nadia had called me yesterday asking why I haven't called her in the three weeks I've been out. I told her I been busy getting my shit together and getting settled in, but reality was, I forgot all about having her number. Now I was on my way to her apartment on this hot afternoon. I got on the Lodge freeway and navigated to the fast lane while I had Jay Z's Reasonable Doubt album filling the void of silence. Ace had just texted me in code, telling me we were running out of heroin. I didn't bother to text him back because I was planning on meeting with Mook today since I've been procrastinating these past few weeks. Hopefully Mook willing to do business with us again.

Twenty minutes later I got off the freeway and pulled up in front of the apartment building. I texted her to let her know I just pulled up, and she replied by telling me to come up to apartment 3-D. I got outta the Beemer and paused to check my attire. I had on a crispy pair of black aviators, and a black diamond rosary. I shoved the new Desert Eagle .45 I just purchased, on my waist fully loaded. I strolled into the building and made my way to the unoccupied elevator, walked up the narrow hallway until I reached Nadia's door, and then rang the doorbell.

Nadia answered the door looking just as sexy as the day I ran into her at the mall. Everything about her was perfect from her short hairstyle to her French tip pedicured toes, and her Baby Phat jeans seemed to fit her perfectly, she clearly looked like she just came from a magazine photo shoot. After taking inventory of her body, I stepped inside.

"What's the science baby girl? You looking spectacular gotta playa thinking about settling down," I said, as I took a look around her one bedroom apartment.

"Yeah whatever boy! You don't even know the definition of settling down, so stop fronting."

"I do know the definition, and it's you. Can I get a hug now?"

I gave her a long tight hug and ended it with a kiss on the cheek, and then we both took a seat on her green couch.

"I'm still mad at you! Talking about you been busy, I should punch you, Gino! And I bet I would've never heard from you if I didn't call you first. What you been busy fucking with them other lame bitches?" asked Nadia, waiting on my response.

I just looked at her for a minute until she moved her neck in a gesture that said 'Say something'. I leaned over and kissed her on her soft, full lips catching her by complete surprise. I sucked on her bottom lip as she wrapped her arms around my neck pulling me closer. She slid her tongue into my mouth and my dick became hard instantly. While we were tongue wrestling I could feel Nadia hands loosening my belt and tugging at my jeans. She reached her hands inside my boxers and stroked my dick firmly, forcing me to become harder. She then pushed me back and stood up with pure seduction in her eyes.

She stripped off her clothes in a record breaking time until she was completely nude. I was too mesmerized at watching her that I only managed to take off my shirt off, but Nadia wasted no time helping me shed my clothes as I stood up in front of the couch. Once I was naked, she wrapped herself in my arms and begins to kiss me again, sucking my tongue as if she was trying to drain it. She pushed me back on the couch and climbed on top of me as I sat up straight. She continued to kiss me and I could feel the heat from her wet pussy hovering above my lap. I grabbed her by her waist and lowered her slowly onto my dick until it disappeared inside of her. She let out a satisfying moan that made my heart skip a beat.

She was so tight and juicy that it felt like her pussy walls were squeezing the blood out of my dick! She slowly gyrated up and down while I palmed both of her ass cheeks and bounced to the rhythm. She knew how to contract her muscle well, and proved it to me every five seconds. Her facial expressions alone could make a porno star erupt quicker than normal. I leaned forward a little bit and started sucking her stiff nipples gently she begin to move faster and moan my name in my ear.

I continued to suck on her nipples while palming her butt, and then I stuck my index finger in her asshole, causing her to scream my name so loud I knew the whole building heard! She rode me even faster, riding me like a thoroughbred stallion. Her juices were dripping off her pussy lips and sliding down my dick all the way to my balls. I could feel the explosion rising inside of me, and she was on the same mission.

"I'm cumming, baby! I'm cumming!" and once those words escaped her lips I could no longer hold it.

I exploded inside of her, and she exploded all over me at the same precise time. We both just sat there trying to catch our breath with my dick still inside her growing soft. I couldn't believe I just fucked this girl raw! I can't let that happen again, I hope she ain't got shit! I was hot, sweaty, and ready to wash the sex aroma off me.

"Oh my god, Gino I hate you! Yelled, Nadia, out of nowhere.

"Damn, why you say that?" I asked, but couldn't stop myself from laughing.

"Because I do! Why you just fuck me raw?" she asked, and I looked at her like she was retarded, I cut the laughing short.

"You just let me fuck you raw, what type of question is that? What type of shit you on...get the fuck off me!" I said, and I gently shoved her off my lap and stood up.

"It's not even like that, Gino. I'm just saying...I don't even know how to say it," Nadia stood up and grabbed my arm as I was putting my boxers on. I snatched away and continued to get dressed.

"Gino, don't be like that! What I'm trying to say is...look I got strong feelings for you, and I don't want you to think I'm a hoe who fucks every nigga I meet. And trust me that's not the case, the only reason I did it with you is because I like you a lot, and I want to be with you."

I looked at Nadia and she had tears in her eyes. I grabbed her and gave her a hug as she cried on my bare chest.

"Stop all that crying, Nadia. I know you far from a hoe; I don't even know why you would say some shit like that. I got genuine love for you girl and I would never try to play you like a random bitch, real talk. I'm going always keep it real with you, and right now is not a good time for us to be together, trust me. But when that time does come, I'll let you know. I got too much on my plate right now, and I'm not ready to jump in no relationship if I'm not going to give it my all."

With that being said, I just held Nadia as she silently cried tears of rejection. If I wasn't with Zaria, then Nadia would most defiantly be my main chick. Lord knows she wifey material that deserved a real nigga to stand by her side. It just couldn't be me.

After leaving that emotional scene at Nadia apartment, I went back to my riverfront condo to take a hot shower. Zaria was at work until later tonight, and that was a good thing because she would've been asking a thousand questions if I came home to take a shower in the middle of the day. And I wasn't even in the mood for that nagging shit. I took a twenty five minute shower, and tried my hardest to get Nadia out of my mind. After drying off, and getting dressed, I sat at my computer and sent my fam Sandman and Jay 100 apiece. I did that every two weeks to let my peeps know I didn't forget about them. They both called me at least twice a week just to hear me talk fly! Real niggaz never forget about their peoples that are behind them gates, so I made sure I kept it one hunnit at all times. After sending my niggaz some money, it was time for me to drive to Taylor to meet Mook. Instead of driving my BMW, I took Zaria's Jeep Liberty so I wouldn't stand out in traffic. I drove in complete silence, no radio, no phone, just my loud thoughts.

I drove up to Mook's quarter-million dollar house parked in the long driveway. My gun was stuffed inside my hoody pocket as I climbed out of the Jeep. I got to the front door and rang the doorbell twice, before Mook answered it with a wide grin on his face.

Muthafucking young Gino! What it do pimp juice?" said Mook, giving me a firm play and hug.

"Ain't shit shaking O.G. Mook. I see you still look like money my baby," I replied, while playfully brushing his shoulders off.

"I'm doing fair for a square youngster, I'm glad to see you finally made it home lil homie. Come on in, we can chill in the living room," Mook closed and locked the door, and I followed him into the living room where a 66 inch plasma T.V. hung from the wall. I took a seat in a lazy boy and Mook sat in a chair across from me. He had an M-16 leaning against his chair, and you could see the bulge from a pistol on his waist.

"What's up with Ace, he ain't fucking with me no more? What he found a better plug?" asked Mook, as he lit up a Newport cigarette.

"Nawl, we ain't got another plug. We just had enough to last us for a hot minute, we almost dry now that's why I'm here today."

"Oh, I thought y'all were done copping from me. He a good businessman and I'll hate to lose him you know y'all like family to me, I watched y'all grow up to be some real money-getters. I'm really proud of y'all boys, but enough of my gratitude, what you trying to snatch up today?"

I leaned in closer to him and begin to speak in a hush tone.

"Look Big Homie, I got half a mil in cash in the Jeep right now as we speak. I know it's chump change to a nigga like you, but I'm uncomfortable carrying that much money around. So tell me what you'll push my way and please don't tell me I gotta wait. I wanna get rid of this money now," I said, looking Mook square in his eyes.

"Nawl baby, you don't have to wait at all, I got whatever you need right here. But could you tell me why we whispering?" asked Mook.

"Because I don't know if anybody else is here, I don't want anybody to know I'm holding that much money, you feel me?"

"Yeah I feel you, but ain't nobody else in the house, it's only me and you my baby. You can walk outta here with the work right now, and I'll cut you a deal. For half a mill, I'll give you-"

Before he could even finish his sentence, I had my .45 in his face, right between his eyes. I reached down and relieved him of his gun tucked in his waist and stuffed it in my hoody pocket.

"Nigga if you make one false move, I'm splattering your education all over the floor. So be smart, don't turn this robbery into a homicide, follow me?" I stated, looking for signs of doubt.

"Straight up Gino! This how you do me? This how you do family! We supposed to be like kinfolks and this-"

I cocked back my arms and smacked him with my pistol; blood started trickling out of his mouth.

"We ain't no fucking family Mook and we never were! What the fuck you mean nigga, you been getting down on my muthafucking brother for the past two years! But I ain't got time to converse about whose real and who's not. You either show me where the money and dope at or die slow, simple once he had the door open he stepped inside and I was directly behind him. The light was already on, and the closet was the size of a gas station bathroom. There were three rows of shelves going around the walls of the whole room stocked with money, bricks of heroin, and guns.

"You can take all this shit Gino, just don't smoke me man. This shit ain't worth my life, don't kill me man," Mook pleaded.

I pulled Mook out of the room and shot him three times in the back of the head! His body slumped to the floor, and blood was all over my face. I wiped the blood, and brain fragments from off my face with the sleeve of my hoody and made sure he still wasn't breathing...

After making sure Mook was dead, I walked back into the closet and noticed a box of black hefty trash bags on the floor. I grabbed one of the bags, and started pushing everything on the bottom shelf into the bag. Once the bag was full, I repeated that until all the shelves were naked. In all, I had five bags that needed to be taken to the jeep. I carried two bags at a time up the stairs and sat them by the front door. After getting all the bags by the front door, I went back down to the basement to wipe clean everything I touched, then went back up to the living room and did the same thing. I grabbed the M-16 and stuffed that in one of the bags. Thinking I covered my tracks, I decided it was time to get the fuck outta here! I unlocked the front door, opened it, and stuck my head out to make sure the coast was clear. Realizing no one was watching me; I grabbed three bags and took them to the Jeep, and stuffed them in the back hatch. I ran back in, grabbed the other two bags placed them in the backseat.

I didn't even bother to close the front door; I just got in the driver's seat, and started the engine up. I had my hand on the shift gear ready to take off until something came to me.

"Those fucking keys," I mumbled, as I got outta the jeep and ran back into the house. I ran to the basement and retrieved the keys I remember touching. I decided to take them with me instead of trying to wipe them off.

This time I closed the front door behind me, got in the car, and calmly backed out of the driveway. I drove off smoothly, making sure not to bring attention to myself. My nerves were just as calm as they were when I walked in the house. My heart never sped up, there was no adrenaline rush, I felt normal as if killing was normal.

Chapter Seven

Gino

Who the fuck does that? Who keeps twenty-five kilos of heroin, and

3 million dollars in cash at the same place he rests his head at?" Asked Ace, still astounded by the major lick I had just pulled off.

"I don't know lil bro; he was slipping like a muthafucka! I guess he thought he was Frank Lucas or somebody. In this game trust is something that's forbidden," I schooled Ace, while I was splitting the three-million in half.

We were at the house in Chesterfield Township, sitting on the couch in the living room. The table was covered with money and the floor was covered with kilos, and an assortment of weapons.

"If we flip those bricks for one hundred thousand apiece that's five million flat! We got five million worth of blow on the floor! You just shitted on that lil lick I hit, I still wish you would've told me, I would've ridden with you for reinforcement."

"I was straight bro; I knew exactly how shit was go play out. If we both would've showed up, he probably would've been on high alert mode, you feel me. You know how you get the bubble guts when you about to ride on a mark or hit a lick? I never got the bubble guts or felt nervous bro I put that on the OG! That's how sure I was about the lick; I just didn't know Mook was holding like that!"

"You ain't never lied! I knew he could get his hands on a few bricks, but I would have never imagined him holding like that. You probably didn't have the bubble guts, but I know that hoe-ass muthafucka Mook shitted on himself!" yelled Ace, falling on the floor laughing.

"You silly as fuck dog! I wouldn't put it past that nigga though, he was crying the whole damn time! I'm thinking 'damn what the babies go do'! But enough about that nigga, what's dead is dead. What's popping with Mitch and Mel? Did that run from Houston go smoothly?"

"Mitch went by himself; I had Mel on anther mission. I can't even tell you if everything went because that bum ain't hit me up yet. He was supposed to touchdown last night, but he didn't answer his phone when I tried to call him," said Ace, checking his phone to see if Mitch called.

"You think he got flicked?" I asked, assuming the very worst.

"If he would've got flicked, Mel would be the first to know, and then Mel would've hit me up. I'll call him again in a minute to see what the business is. We gotta move all these guns and dope to one of the stash houses tonight around midnight; we can't leave this shit here. We hitting up the Zoo Bar tonight, we deserve to take a break and have a good time."

"I really ain't with the club shit bro, that's more of your speed. I'll just lay back with the wifey tonight and relax," I replied, not even in the mood to be in a crowded place with a bunch of rowdy young thugs.

"Come on bro, you gotta pop bottles with us! We might as well say we're millionaire's baby! It's time to celebrate our wealth, and then we can get back on the grind. But tonight you gotta fuck with ya lil homie," Ace practically begged.

"Aight, aight damn! We go ball out tonight, but like you said tomorrow its politics as usual," I gave in to Ace pleading and decided to have a little fun for once.

I finally finished splitting the money in a half and pushed 1.5 million towards Ace. It was an odd 100 bill that I put to the side, I picked it up and grabbed a lighter that was sitting on the table, and set the 100 bill on fire. I twirled it for a few seconds before laying it in the ashtray.

"What the fuck you burning money for?!" asked Ace.

"We split everything down the middle; never can we let anything come between us no matter how much money we make. That 100 bill symbolize everything I just said, since it was an odd bill I would rather burn it than keep it," we stood up and I gave my little brother a hug.

66

I meant every word I just said, and I prayed that Ace felt the same way. The bible said money was the root of all evil for a reason, because I witnessed the malice money cause between the best of friends. It's like I can't trust a dude that says money over everything. By saying its money over everything means nothing is above the almighty dollar so you'll go to great lengths to get it and keep it. Family, friends, and life are unimportant to that individual, only money. I was never one of those types of dudes, money is meaningless to me, and money doesn't love anybody. And once niggaz realize that, disloyalty wouldn't be at an all-time high.

"Oh yeah, that ain't shit but 1.5 million, that's pocket change you can splurge with, just make sure you spend it all," we both smiled and stared at the pile of money laid across the table.

We came a long way from living on welfare, I never seen or touched this much money in my entire life! But I had the demeanor as if this was an everyday thing.

We pulled up to the club six cars deep, all foreign whips. It was ten of us altogether, everybody was riding two deep except for me. We decided to treat everybody we had on the payroll which was Mitch, Mel, Murda, Prodigy, Snoop, A.J., Chris, and Smurf. Murda and Smurf were my homies that I brought into our circle that I trusted with my life. I met them both in prison at I-Max level 5 back in 2000 when we all went to war with some Aryan Nation crackers. We punished them racist bitches in the law library, then we all went to segregation. Ever since then we have been tight.

Murda was exactly what his name was, a straight killah. He did 10 years for involuntary manslaughter he caught back when he was only 17 years old. He was down to ride for whatever, that's why I hooked up with him a few weeks ago and brought him into our family.

Now Smurf was a pretty boy type of guy until he was dead and gone. He did a 3 year sentence, and didn't do as much as one push-up! Every time we asked him why he didn't workout he always told us, 'I look too good to workout'. We use to laugh our ass off! But don't let that pretty boy shit fool you, he's a thoroughbred dude that will get grimy in a split second.

Now Mitch, Mel, Prodigy, Chris, A.J., and Snoop were all Ace homies he was fucking with before I came home. He was close to Mitch and Mel, who were twins and they seemed solid to me. But when I look at them I can sense that they are somewhat intimidated by my presence, especially Mitch. You can never trust scary niggaz! The other dudes were strictly workers, nothing more nothing less.

I hopped out of my Beemer looking like and feeling like a million dollars. After all I was worth more than a million dollars so I had the right to feel and look how I pleased! We walked straight into the club, passing the long line, and gave the bouncer a stack to keep the searching to the next person. Fine women were everywhere, right along with a flock of hating niggaz.

You could feel the bass from the music through the floor, and the females were either dancing, or swaying to the music trying to look cute and not sweat. As usual, the females were breaking their necks to get a glimpse at me, and it was obvious to those on the outside looking in. I had on a pair of Red Monkeys, a white T-shirt, a pair of cream and white Louis Vuitton gym shoes, and my jewelry game was ridiculous! I went to the Jewelry Factory in Livonia and spent close to ninety thousand on a VVS 30 carat diamond chain, it looked like a glass of ice water around my neck. Not to mention the custom made Joe Rodeo 6 carat canary yellow diamond flooded face and wristband I only paid twenty stacks for. But the most important accessory I was wearing was a Glock .17 on my hip. A pistol is a necessity in this type of environment, and all ten of us were strapped and ready for any misunderstanding.

We made our way to the V.I.P section where all the money getting hustlers were located spending plenty money. We were then escorted to two tables that seated five people. After taking our seats, a waitress appeared to take our orders. She was a cute, petite light-skinned chick, but nothing worth calling home over.

"Hello gentleman, my name is Destiny and I'm your waitress for the night. Can I get you anything?" she asked, with a surprisingly addictive smile.

I reached in my pocket and pulled out ten grand and counted out five of it, then placed the other five back in my pocket. I gave her the stack of money forcing her smile to become wider than before, but I ignored the change of emotion and remained humble.

"Listen, Destiny is it?" I asked.

"Yes, it's Destiny, and your name is?" she asked me in return.

"My name is Gino, and it's a pleasure to meet you," I responded, giving her a gentle handshake. She couldn't help but to blush.

"Now listen cutie, I want you to take that five racks and peel away from it as we order whatever we desire. If we surpass that budget you are holding, let me know and I'll lace you again. If the math is accurate when we're ready to exit, I'll be sure to leave you a healthy tip. In fact…," I paused to reach in my pocket and peel off five-hundred dollars." Take this, it's yours. Just make sure the ice cubes never melt. Right now you can bring us ten bottles of Dom P."

"Alright Mr. Gino, I'll be right back," she turned to walk away but I grabbed her wrist to stop her. She turned back around to face me, and she looked down at her wrist.

"Gino…just call me Gino," she smiled seductively and went to get our drinks once I released her wrist.

"You swear you got game, Gino! You need to realize you're not me, and then you'll sleep better!" said Smurf, causing us all to laugh.

While everybody was conversing I was looking around observing my surrounding. A couple of dope boys nodded at me with respect when I caught eye contact with them, and I nodded back. A group of females were looking over at our tables, some smiled and waved so I gave them the same nod I gave the dope boys. These gold-digging bitches were looking for a meal ticket, and I wasn't passing them out!

Destiny finally came back with our champagne with the aide of another waitress, sat the bottle in the ice buckets, and retreated back to her work station. We all grabbed a bottle and popped it open, spilling champagne in the process.

"I really ain't a give a speech type of guy, but I gotta give this toast to my big brother. He fresh out the joint and he right back on the grind, welcome back bruh I needed you out here with me. It's time to live life, stack paper, and prosper to greater heights. We go make it to the top but the question is who's going to be up there with us when it's all said and done? Its death before dishonor my niggaz, and we live by that, ain't no turning back no matter what! Tonight we here to take a break and enjoy ourselves, but tomorrow it's back to business. I'm gonna need y'all to hold y'all bottles in the air for my brother, come on put them fucking bottles up! We run this shit, why you bullshitting we can buy this fucking club!" everybody start tapping bottles with each other and drank straight from the bottle, fuck a champagne flute!

As the fellas kicked it and joked, I was in my own world. I wasn't comfortable sitting in a packed club with all eyes on us, but I had to keep reminding myself I was here for Ace. He wanted to celebrate, so that's what we did, we weren't hiding from the Red Mayfia or nobody else! As I was deep in my own thoughts, I heard somebody calling my name.

"Aye Gino! Gino! I turned around in my seat, hand resting on the pistol on my hip. I zoomed in on where the voice was coming from and spotted a tall Cat with his hands in the air as if he was signaling a field gold.

"Who the fuck is that bro?" Murda asked me.

"I don't even know, just be on point," I replied, not taking my eyes off the approaching stranger. As he got closer he started to look familiar.

"Man...fall back Murda, everything cool, that's my homie Lo-Lo," I stood up from my seat after taking another sip of the Dom P...

"My nigga Gino, grimy ass eastside hustler!" said Lo-Lo, as we embraced each other with brotherly love.

"Lo-Lo, what it is my dude? Long time no see, what's been going on with you?" I asked, looking Lo-Lo over carefully and it was obvious he was getting money. His Armani attire, and rose gold chain spoke for itself.

"Ain't too much going on with me my baby. Welcome home boy, it's good to see you back in the city! I had been meaning to call you, I just been busy as fuck."

"Who you get my number from?" I asked, knowing the answer to my own question. Lo-Lo looked at me with a smirk on his face.

"You know where I got the fucking number from, so stop fronting! And I don't appreciate you fucking my lil cousin either."

"Who said I fucked her?"

"Come on Gino, she been in love with you since she was young as fuck! She told me you stopped by her apartment yesterday, so I know you smashed. I ain't tripping though, she a grown ass woman now, do what you do."

"Lo-Lo I ain't need your permission with your overprotective ass!" everybody laughed at my comment but I was dead serious.

"I see y'all deep as fuck in here. What up Ace? You act like you don't know a real muthafucka!" said Lo-Lo, directing his attention to Ace.

"What's good homie? Where the fuck you been hiding at?" asked Ace, as he gave Lo-Lo some dap.

"I went to the joint for 2 years on a felony weapon case, I been out for about a year now."

"You were in the joint?" I asked, clearly surprised.

"Fuck yeah! Nadia didn't tell you?"

"Hell nawl! I asked her why you ain't get at me while I was gone and all she said was 'I don't know, ask him'."

"I wanted to pop at you but I was out here fucked up, doing real bad bro. I was broke and too ashamed to write you and not send a dime, and that's on my dead granny! Then I got hit with that case, and I did 8 months in the country before I got sentenced. They let me out last year, and I was still struggling, hitting petty licks. A few months ago, I hit a gravy lick! I'll put you up on it later, fam I even own a pool hall on Woodward."

"That's what's up, I'm glad you finally on your feet. You here with somebody?" I asked, noticing we were still standing up.

"I met somebody up here to handle some business, but they gone now. I came up here trying to find a bad bitch to take back to the Best Western," Lo-Lo started looking around the V.I.P.

"You might as well post up with us for a minute and sip on something, my treat," I offered as we sat down, and I waved Destiny over to order more bottles.

74

We sat there for a couple hours sipping bottle after bottle, enjoying each other's company. Everybody cracked jokes, telling prison stories that were exaggerated to a certain extent, and just had a plain old good time. Ace even invited some females to join us at our table, but I wasn't even giving my attention to one of them, I really wasn't impressed. I was on my third bottle buzzing like a muthafucka! Ace and I were discussing the next car we planned to purchase when I felt a vibe that somebody was staring at me. I slightly turned to my right and scanned the scene, and my eyes met with a young, brown-skinned, stocky built, short thug dressed in red and black. He was seated at a table with two other young gangsta that looked no more than 18 years old, and four provocatively dressed woman drinking shots of Grey Goose. I held eye contact with him for a few seconds, and then he looked away and begin conversing with one of the females.

"Gino…Gino," Ace called me as he shook my shoulder.

"Bro stop touching me! What's good?" I responded, knocking Ace hand off my shoulder.

"What the fuck is you staring at, you straight?" asked Ace, sensing something was wrong.

"I'm kosher. Somebody looked familiar, that's all," I looked over at the youngin again and he was still indulged in a conversation with the same female. This Dom P. had me tweaking!

"Hey my peeps y'all ready to blow this bitch? I don't know about y'all but I'm ready to dive in some pussy!" I announced, as I checked the time but could barely see it due to the diamonds forcing me to squint. Everybody felt the same as me, so I signaled the waitress over to our tables.

"What can I do for you Gino?" asked Destiny.

"We ready to slide outta here now, it's getting late. You can bring me the bill please," I said, in a polite matter.

I was somewhat feeling Destiny, I just didn't know what intrigued me about her. I mean she was cute, and had a nice body, but them two pluses aren't the most important factors to me. I was more attracted to a woman intellect; I thrived off potent conversation, and was aroused by philosophic point of views. She walked off to get the bill, and came back thirty seconds later with it in her hand.

"Your total is thirty-three hundred, you gave me a five thousand tab, so here's your change which adds up to seventeen-hundred," she placed the money in the palm of my hand, and I sat it on the table without counting it. I had already done the math in my head before I requested the bill and her math was accurate. I reached in my pocket and peeled off 300 from a knot of money, and added it with the seventeen-hundred, making it an even two grand. I extended my hand and held out the two stacks for to take.

"This is your tip for doing such a great job tonight, lil mama. I really appreciate your service," I said, with such convictions that she blessed me with her radiant smile once again.

"I can't accept that big of a tip, I'm only doing my job!" said Destiny, taking a step back from the table as if she was scared of the money.

"I insist, please don't refuse my generosity. To me you did more than your job and I wanna show my appreciation," I continued to hold the money out for her to take but she wouldn't budge.

"I'm sorry I don't mean to seem ungrateful, but as much as I would like to take that money, I can't."

"Okay I'll give you two choices, but you have to pick one, okay?" I asked, and she hesitantly shook her head yes.

"Either you accept my tip, or you accept my invitation to be friends, and let me treat you to dinner sometime this week," I offered and she batted her eyelashes, trying her hardest not to seem overexcited.

"I think I'll accept your second offer," she replied

"Is it against policy to flirt with customers?" I teased her

"Excuse me! No it's not. Why did you ask that, do you think I'm flirting with you?" she asked, raising her right eyebrow.

"No I don't think you're flirting with me, I know you are!" She laughed at my comment, and I knew then I had her nose open.

"Do you have a phone you can store my number in because I'm tired of you making me blush in front of all my peoples who happens to be thugs, so how do you think that makes me look?" I joked, and Destiny laughed again at my sarcastic humor.

"You are so crazy, and no I don't have my phone, it's in my car charging. But I can go grab a pen real quick," she offered.

"Nawl, don't even worry about it. Aye Smurf let me get your phone, " Smurf passed me his phone and I erased all of his stored phone numbers, text messages, and all personal information, then I saved my phone number into the phone.

"Here, you can keep this phone. Don't worry about the bill, I'll take care of it, all I ask of you is don't give that number to anybody else. I want to be the only person that can call you on that phone, that way it's no excuse why you ain't answer it. Is That cool with you lil mama"?

"I guess it's cool, but I see you're very outgoing with everything you do."

"I'm a generous man, what can I say?"

"Don't say nothing, just be sure to call me," she replied, in a very seductive way.

"You need not to even remind me, I might call you as soon as I get outside!" I joked, and this time when she laughed she put her hand on my shoulder.

"You are so silly!"

"I love to see your smile, I wanna continue to see it, so be prepared to smile hard whenever I'm around. I would love to sit here and talk to you until the sun rise, but I gotta get up in the morning," I stood up and sat the money on the table while keeping eye contact with Destiny. I wrapped my arms around Destiny and gave her a firm hug, and planted a kiss on her cheek. Without saying another word I begin to walk away leaving her standing there in a trance, feenin for my presence. I looked back to see her still staring at me as if it would be her last time seeing me.

"Don't forget to get your tip off the table, you deserve it and much more," before she could protest, I disappeared into the large crowd and was bumped kind of aggressively. I mugged the clown that bumped me and it just so happen to be the same young punk I thought was mugging me dressed in red and black!

"My fault blood," he mumbled and kept walking.

I looked at him for a few seconds and he vanished from my line of sight. These younginz ain't got any respect that's exactly why I didn't wanna hit the club in the first place! I glanced over at Murda and he was in militant mode as usual, his hand buried under his shirt gripping his pistol. We continued to exit the club together with Lo-Lo on one side of me and Ace on the other. Once we made it outside, the front of the club was just as packed as the inside of it! Everybody was illegally parked in the streets with their sound systems banging, and big rims shining trying to attract any bitch that was ready to get busted open. It was barely enough room to move your arms; I had to hurry up and get the fuck in my car.

"Yo Lo-Lo, you staying in the city tonight?" I asked

"Hell yeah! Me and shorty right here on our way to a room. I got some more business to take care of tomorrow and then I'm shooting back to 'Ypsi'. I want to sit down with you sometime tomorrow and discuss making money together, so I'm go chirp you after I handle my other business." Just as I was about to open my mouth and respond, I spotted that young nigga in red and black with several other niggaz scanning the crowd as if they were searching for an enemy. He stopped looking once he spotted me, and tapped his homeboy next to him pointing directly at me. They begin to push themselves through the crowd aggressively, and without hesitating I pulled out my Glock .17, and held it to my side. Ace and Lo-Lo noticed my gesture and without asking questions pulled out their tools.

"What the fuck you doing G-...," before Ace could finish his sentence I fired two shots in the young niggaz direction once I seen the reaching

80

for their waist. Everybody that I came with ducked down and pulled out their pistols as innocent people were screaming and running for safety.

The young niggaz who were all clad in red and black, returned fire at us and backed away at the same time like they planned on making a run for it. We ducked behind our expensive cars and shot right back at them, watching as one dropped to the ground bleeding. My heart was beating in overdrive and all I was worried about was all the witnesses that could fry a nigga if ever we get caught and make it to that courtroom! Murda was the closes to them, and he was standing behind his car shooting over the roof, not even bothering to duck! Murda had some real mental issues, but I expected that out of him. I stop shooting and looked around to make sure everybody I came with was counted for, but Lo-Lo and Smurf were nowhere in sight! I know these muthafucka's ain't just run on us and leave us for dead! I had no time to worry about them, I knew we had to make a quick getaway before the police showed up and joined the party. I lifted back up and let off a few accurate shots before sliding back to the ground for cover.

BOOM! BOOM! BOOM!

Goddamn, what the fuck is they shooting?! It sounded like somebody decided to put the handgun down and picked up some heavy artillery! I looked over to make sure Ace was straight, and he was staring at me with the same confused expression. I looked the other way and Murda was not only still standing, but now walking towards the young niggaz still aiming and shooting. I stood up just in time to see one of Murda bullets rip through the head of one of them, killing him instantly. I looked past the bodies that were sprawled out on the cement to see Lo-Lo and Smurf standing with matching Mossberg pistol-grip pumps,

We all heard the sirens closing in on us, and everybody ran for their car. I hurriedly got in my BMW, which was now riddled with bullet holes, and sped off in haste.

Chapter 8

Gino

The next day I woke with a foggy mind due to all the champagne I consumed last night at the club. My ears still ringing from all the gunshots that threaten to take my life. I can't continue to live life worried about who was the next to try to leave my brains on the ground. Something had to change because next time we might not be that lucky. These wanna be gangstas had no concern for all the innocent bystanders!

Me, and Ace went to my condo after the shooting since it was way closer than his house. Luckily, only one person got shot out of our entourage, Chris took a bullet to his arm but it was nothing tragic. Lo-Lo drove him out to a hospital in Ypsilanti to avoid being linked to the club shooting. At first I thought Lo-Lo and Smurf took off on us, but it turned out they were around the block to Lo-Lo truck to grab the Mossberg's, and snuck up behind the lil niggaz. The element of surprise helped us walk away from that bloody scene alive; I owe them two niggaz until I'm dead!

I knew the Red Mafiya was behind that hit, it was something about that lil muthafucka that had me on high alert, and his actions exposed his intentions. All that mugging and then him bumping me told me he was up to something so I kept my eyes on him. Anybody can shoot a pistol, but it takes a real man to strategize a plan and execute without being sloppy. Those lil bastards weren't smart enough for war and now they were dead because of their lack of intelligence, but that's how the game goes. I had a feeling the streets were on fire, swarming with homicide detectives. I just pray none of our names pop up!

I got out of the bed and noticed that Zaria was not in the bed with me. The clock read 10:00 am, which was kind of early for her to be up on her work days. I staggered to the bathroom to take a long piss, and brush my teeth. After leaving the bathroom and walking out to the hallway, the smell of breakfast filled the air sparking my stomach to growl. Zaria was in the kitchen standing over the stove, and Ace was sitting at the kitchen island indulged in a deep conversation on his phone. I tapped him on the back as I walked past him toward my baby, and gave her a kiss on the lips.

"Good morning sleepy-head, it's nice you finally decided to join us. I was just about to wake you up after I finished the pancakes," said Zaria, diverting her attention back to the stovetop. I went and sat on a stool next to Ace.

"That champagne drained all my energy, I'm done drinking. It smells good in here, what's the occasion?" I asked jokingly.

"The occasion is you still being alive," replied Zaria, with a major attitude.

"What the fuck are you talking about, lil mama?" I said, acting as if I was confused but knew exactly what she was referring too.

"I'm talking about the same thing the newspapers, and the news casters are talking about, the big shooting at the club last night!"

"I don't know what the hell you talking about so pipe down with all that hype shit."

"So you mean Ace lying to me? I know some niggaz came and got your car this morning!"

I looked at Ace with a disappointing look on my face. Why would he tell her some shit like that?

"Why the fuck you tell her that shit nigga?" I asked him.

"Nigga I ain't tell her shit. I had somebody steal your car and destroy it and she wanted to know why, but I didn't tell her nothing. I guess she watched the news, put two and two together, and figured we were involved in the shooting. So technical you just told on yourself buddy," exclaimed Ace, as he covered the mouthpiece on his phone so whoever he was talking to couldn't hear him.

I looked over at Zaria and she was standing with her hands on her hips, shaking her head at my slip up.

"I see you think you inspector gadget or some shit. Fix me a plate, I'm hungry as fuck," I demanded.

"So you not gone tell me what happened last night?"

"It ain't none of your damn business what happen, stay in your place is what you need to do!"

"It is my business if my man about to lose his freedom or life! Don't make me leave you Gino!" Zaria threatened.

"Something wrong with your leg? Your feet don't look broke to me, you wanna leave then get the fuck on!" she didn't bother to reply, she just continued to make the pancakes.

"Ace, I need to talk to you, get the fuck off the phone," Ace held his index finger up indicating for me to wait a minute.

Zaria made us all a plate stacked with pancakes, bacon, sausages, eggs, and hash browns. I took a bite of the bacon just as Ace ended his phone call.

"Why the fuck y'all doing all that yelling while I'm on the phone?" asked Ace, taking a bite of his bacon.

"Mind your own business Ace. Zaria, can you eat in the bedroom while we discuss business?"

"What? You get on my fucking nerves boy! We ain't purchase this condo for office space, you want to discuss business lease a damn business office and discuss business there!" yelled Zaria, as she stormed off to the bedroom.

"I love you baby!" I screamed back playfully.

"Fuck you Gino!" she screamed back before slamming the bedroom door.

Me and Ace couldn't stop ourselves from laughing.

"On some serious shit bro, what the fuck is our next move? We can't keep having these fake gangsta's shooting at us any given time," I said taking another bite of food.

"Yeah, I feel you my baby. I'm ready to go to war even though I know the chances of winning are slim to none! I think if we take out the leader, the rest of them chump's go fold camp," said Ace, but I shook my head in disagreement and swallowed a mouthful of food before speaking.

"That's not true with every organization or gang bro, bloods are different they move different, and if we manage to clap Slime them bitches killing everything moving! Once Slime dies another nigga go take his place before his body makes it to the hospital. And by the time they pronounce him dead, one of us want make it to the next day. I'm not saying that they untouchable, all I'm saying is we need to weigh our pros and cons, is it worth losing our life of doing life?"

"I understand, but something needs to shake or this shit will never cease until I'm dead. I'm not paying him all that money so that's dead. I'll pay him back what I took with a lil interest, but that's it. Slime ain't about to extort me, so he can forget it," said Ace, too upset to eat anymore.

"I'll go meet up with Slime today; we need to come up with some type of agreement or something."

"Gino is you crazy! Dog, you not about to meet with that dude, he liable to snatch you up on sight!" Ace was shocked at my decision to meet Slime face to face, but what other solution did we have?

"Well lil bro, that's a chance I'll have to take. But he wouldn't get me like that, we done been through too much together. I'll make him give me his word on neutral grounds. Was the club shooting all over the news?" I asked Ace, changing the subject.

"Fuck yeah! Four of Slime Goons was dead, and one was in critical condition. Lo-Lo and Smurf laid them boys out when they snuck up on them from behind. The news said they had no leads so far, but you know how close they play it. My homie Brent, cool with the owner of the club, and I called him as soon as I took off from the scene. I told him to make sure that shooting surveillance video never touch the police hand, he said he wanted ten thousand, so I had Mitch take him the money and pick up the tape. I told Mitch to destroy the tape ASAP, can't take no more chances holding on to it so we should be good. Ain't no witnesses, no video, and no suspects so far. I had one of my peeps steal your whip and take it to the junk yard free of charge. We all took a lost but it ain't shit, cars come and go."

"What's the news on your lil homie Chris?" I asked.

'Chris good, he only got hit in the arm, it went straight through. Him and Lo-Lo should be back in the city by 2 o'clock, he said he go chirp you when he touchdown. But what's up with your man's Murda?! Is that dude retarded, I see this cat standing up shooting and dodging bullets like he was in a fucking action movie!" yelled Ace, as he reenacted the way Murda was dodging bullets.

"My man's a real goon! He doesn't give a fuck. He ain't got it all bro. I was ducked down looking at the nigga in amazement, but hey he ain't catch a bullet and I seen him spill at least two of them fuck boys. He definitely a soldier, that's why I fuck with him," I finished eating and sat my empty plate in the sink.

"I know you don't like the idea of me going to meet up with Slime on some solo shit, but trust me I'll be kosher. Either we make peace, or we gotta get ready for a war. Make sure Mitch got rid of that tape, and stop putting so much trust in that nigga, he seem too timid to me."

"Man, he solid Gino. He ain't gonna cross me, the consequences ain't worth it," replied Ace, still taking bites of his bacon.

"If you say so, that's your mans. I'm getting ready to take a shower, and then swerve through the hood. You got Slime number don't you?" I asked.

"Yeah, I got it," he picked up his phone and strolled through his contacts.

"Good, text it to me right quick. What you got planned for today?"

"Shit, I'm about to catch a cab to the crib and order a rental. I still gotta move all the bricks and guns to the stash house. I might have to take a chance and transport that shit in broad day. And you know what time it is if that meeting with Slime don't go right," said Ace giving me a serious look.

"Yeah I already know. I got my Flint connect on speed dial, I just hope it don't come to that. I'm busy trying to get money, not catch a murder case. I'll hit you up after I talk to dog, if I don't call you by 6 o'clock, come looking for me."

******

I pulled up to the corner of Wade and Newport in Zaria's Jeep Liberty by my lonesome. The only thing that accompanied me was the P90 Ruger with an extended clip. I had to get rid of the Glock .17 from last night, I didn't want to get caught with that hot muthafucka.

I called Slime back when I was at the condo and we agreed to meet on the block we grew up on. So many memories invaded my mind with different emotions. We had good times on this very block, we had fights on this very block, we hustled on this very block, and some of my homies died on this very block. I put the car in park once I seen a red 2004 Corvette ZR1 parked on the opposite side of the street with a licensed plate that read: Soo Woo. I looked up and down the street to see if there was anybody else. I got out of the Jeep and walked towards the Corvette casually.

Slime maneuvered out of the coupe and brushed his Billionaire Mafia shirt and pants off. He had on no flashy jewelry, he just wore a David Yurman watch, and a five-point star red diamond ring on his wedding ring finger. Nothing much changed in his appearance; he looked the same as he did 10 years ago. He was tall maybe 6'2, slim but clearly cut up, really no facial hair just a light mustache, 360 waves, and straight white teeth that looked as if he had dental work done. Growing up I wouldn't have thought Slime would be a founder of a blood gang with over 500,000 members nationwide, and grossed multi-millions yearly. I mean he always hustled growing up to keep up with the latest trend, but we were all victims of poverty. Slime went to prison for 6 years, and once he got out he was on a mission to come up. He met the right connects in the joint and made his dreams come true. We was once closer than brothers with the same mother but different fathers, that's why I didn't understand why he would try to play Ace like that.

"Wade boy Gino, what it like my peoples? Welcome home boy, I'm glad you made it out of the trenches in one piece," said Slime as he embraced me with a genuine hug.

"What's good Slime, I see you doing big things my baby. How the family doing? What's up with Boogie and Zeke?"

"The family tree strong as ever. Boogie will be home soon and Zeke tight he is laying back waiting to bleed on these streets. How your peoples doing?" he asked with a hint of sincerity.

"That's why I came to meet you today."

"I guess we came to talk about Ace, huh?" asked Slime, with an amused smirk on his face.

"Slime you on some straight bullshit-," before I could complete my statement, he cut me off.

"Listen blood, I got unconditional love and respect for you, Ace, and your whole family. I been knowing y'all for forever and a day, but when it comes to my money...," he paused for a second and looked deep

92

into my soul,"…I don't discriminate no matter how much love I got for that individual."

"I understand that, but you know Ace didn't know that he was stealing from you when he robbed dog-"

"I don't know shit, and I really don't give a fuck! But the moment I gave him that option to live, he should've taken it without hesitation. He's getting plenty money in my city, and I don't even tax him to hustle on my streets, everybody else I tax them like Uncle Sam! But since he wants to let his nuts hang and be grown, I'm go treat him like he grown. If you were smart-," Slime was cut off by the sound of his passenger door opening, a sexy Italian female got out of the car looking good enough to be Miss America.

"Daddy, your phone is ringing do you want me to bring it to you?" asked the beautiful goddess.

"No don't worry about it baby girl. But say hello to an old friend of mine. Gino this is Angelina, Angelina this is Gino-"

"Man fuck that bitch!" I blurted out clearly agitated. "We talking about some serious shit and you wanna pretend everything sweet!"

The woman looked at me in confusion, and Slime had the same stupid smirk on his face, satisfied that I lost my cool.

"Don't worry about it baby, just get in the car," she followed his instructions without protesting and got back in the car but her emerald green eyes never looked away from me.

"Don't be so disrespectful!" joked Slime, but I didn't crack a smile.

"I ain't in a playing mood, Slime."

"On some serious shit you need to be careful who you call bitch, because that bitch you just disrespected got more bodies under her belt than I do," said Slime, with an assured shake of his head.

"We need to come up with some type of agreement and squash this nonsense between us," I said with a calm voice, but slightly uneasy from finding out the sexy woman he was with actually killed people.

"I already told y'all the proposal, but I'll state it again for good measures. I want twenty-five thousand monthly for the next 5 years. But since your home and I am happy that you're home, just give me twenty thousand monthly for the next 5 years, and then everyone is alive and happy."

"Come on that's not a fair compromise! How do you know we can afford to pay that much, that's over a million dollars altogether. It's not reasonable even if you drop it to twenty thousand dollars, that's still way too much and it's only a fifty thousand dollar deduction," I said, doing the math in my head.

"That's the best I can do for you blood. I know one thing for sure though; your brother is hard man to kill. I done buried seven shooters behind that nigga-wait-what happen to lil Joe?" asked Slime.

"Who is Lil Joe?"

"My soldier in training you caught breaking into Zaria's house."

"Oh, that's his name? He dead," I replied.

"Wonderful. So let's do the math, the attempt kidnapping at Zaria's house, and the club shooting last night, seven of my men were killed altogether. And Ace selfishness was the cause of all this. And guess who gotta pay for all these funerals, that's right I do! I'm losing money and goons' fucking with your brother, as a matter of fact the price is going back up, twenty-five thousand monthly!" announced Slime, shaking his head in disbelief.

"Nigga we only killed Lil Joe, and four foot soldiers at the club. I know I shot that scary bitch that was with Lil Joe but I ain't known I killed him too," I said, stunned at the discovery.

"You didn't I did once he told me what happened. And we just took a trip down to St. John's hospital and magically turned that critical condition survivor from last night to deceased. They all just a casualty of war, luckily I get a discount at Swanson's Funeral Home," Slime paused and pointed at my waist.

"What kind of banger is that? Whatever it is it got an extended clip on it, maybe thirty shots. You weren't planning to kill me were you? But never mind that, you try to talk some sense into your brother and then call me. Until then he'll be looking over his shoulder until he's kneeling before me. I don't want you, just him even though I know you go ride with him until the bloody end. I would love to go back down memory lane with you but I'm a very busy man, and I know my soldiers tired of being ducked off watching our conversation," I start looking around, but didn't see a soul.

I turned my focus back on Slime and he was smiling from ear to ear.

"You can't see them but they most definitely see you. I never move without them, remember that. One blood, my baby," and with that said, Slime got in his Corvette, and I walked back to the Jeep feeling like I accomplished nothing.

After I got in and started the Jeep up, Slime pulled up next to me and rolled down his window. I rolled down my window to see what else he had to say that we didn't cover.

"On some serious shit Gino, tell Ace to buy you a real automobile! He making all this money and he got you riding around in some shit that looks stolen! Since I feel some type of pity on you, I'll drop the payment back down to twenty grand monthly. If you looking for work holla at me ASAP blood!" said Slime, then he sped off burning rubber in the process.

"Arrogant sonofabitch".

Chapter Nine

Gino

Two months had passed since I had that brief and frivolous meeting with Slime, and nobody attempted to kill Ace. We had been hustling as if every day was our last on earth, and the money was coming in abundance once I flipped half of the heroin I robbed Mook for. I ran the heroin business and was pushing it by the weight, managing to gross 2.5 million in a two month time frame.

Ace, Mitch, and Mel was pushing at least twenty bricks of Caine every two weeks. Really Mitch and Mel was doing all of the footwork like taking trips down to Houston, also transporting the product back to the city. Ace had been staying out of the limelight by not showing his face in public. He even rented a low-key minivan with tented windows to maneuver through traffic in without being noticed; he put on hold all of his club hopping, and dinning at popular restaurants. I was glad he finally realized the severity of the situation we were in with the Red Mafiya, it also helped me sleep a little better at night.

Other then moving my product, I've been enjoying the fruits of my labor. I cashed out on a new 2004 Aston Martin through a broker I retained; only paying 75% of the asking price. The car was in his name so I didn't have to worry about the IRS all in my business. Since the Aston was attracting too much attention, I bought a 2004 Audi A7 through the broker too, which I drove daily. The money was plentiful, plus I still had 1.5 million I could spend on whatever, so the two cars didn't budge my pockets.

Zaria and I were still madly in love; I was fucking her every day as if I just came home a few hours ago. I was still seeing Nadia on the side, but it was hard to keep emotions out of our equation. I couldn't quite put a finger on it, but it was something about Nadia that had me falling in love with her every time we made eye contact. She was definitely wifey material then again I couldn't wife her, or mislead her into believing she was my woman when I had a woman I went home to every night. I wanted to tell her I wasn't ready to be in a relationship. Maybe I'll tell her when the time was right, until then I was going to continue to be in her life.

Lo-Lo and I started doing business with each other everything was looking up so far. Lo-Lo had Ypsilanti on lock with the Caine, and ecstasy pills. Since it was somewhat of a drought on the heroin in his city, I opened up five 'dog food' houses up his way, them bitches was doing numbers! Unlike Detroit where I sold 100 a gram, in his city a gram was going for 120. I had Murda control my houses in Ypsilanti since I had plenty of business to tend to in my own city. Ever since Lo-Lo opened his arms to me in his town, I returned the favor to him by letting him open some pill houses on the eastside. Our enterprise was doing well; the money was steady flowing so I had to move my Flint murder squad to Detroit so they could be close to me when I needed them. I had to send them to Ypsilanti to get rid of a few cats who didn't agree with my setting up shop in there hood. Once that misunderstanding was resolved, and the demonstration was laid down, I gained the respect needed to get money without being tested by some arrogant wanna be thug who had no hustling ambition. However, that type of situation comes with the game, you just have to keep your eyes open and mouth closed.

At the moment I was at Nadia's apartment, stretched out on the couch with her watching an episode of Family Guy. I had 1.2 million in cash inside a Nike duffel bag sitting behind the couch. I was getting ready to take that money to Slime first thing in the morning, and I decided to stash the money here until then. That's right, I was paying Slime what he wanted rather Ace liked it or not. I mean we had plenty of money so why not pay it and put an end to the beef between us and the Red Mafiya. Like I told Ace when I first came home, we can't beef and get money at the same time! I was about getting money and didn't care who thought I was a coward for paying Slime to dead our issues. I see it as I was saving both of our lives by doing what's smart. Besides, the money was coming out of my stash and it was chump change in my eyes.

"Nadia wake ya snoring ass up," I joked as I shook her awake.

"Whhaaat! Boy, stop shaking me I bet you don't even want anything". She said in an aggravated tone.

"Shut the fuck up with all that complaining, and wake yo hot mouth ass up!" I joked and then shoved her playfully off my lap.

"Stoooop! You gone make me fall, Gino!"

"Well move so I can get ready to go."

"I thought you said you were staying the night?"

"You thought wrong, because I said no such thing. As much as I would love to stay, I got business to take care of."

"Business my ass Gino, you probably got some bitch you got lined up ready to fuck. You don't need to lie to me; we're not married or committed."

"Thank you for acknowledging that, so with that being said, I don't need to explain shit to you anymore about my whereabouts," I got up from the couch, and put my shoes on.

"Nooo, I'm sorry baby!" She said as if she was a toddler. "I won't complain again, I'm sorry. I just hate when you leave me here alone," she protested as she stood up and wrapped her arms around me.

I'm not tripping; I already know what it is. All I'm saying is I spend as much time with you as I can, and that still ain't enough! When I tell you I'm going to handle some business, that's exactly what the fuck I'm going to do," I kissed her on the forehead and let her go to put on my shirt.

"I understand baby, when are you coming back?" she asked with a pouty look on her face.

"I'll be back in the morning to pick up that money. Can I trust you enough to leave it here without you getting any fucked up ideas?"

"What type of question is that?"

"The type of question I want answered," I shot back in a serious tone.

""I can't believe you would ask me some shit like that. You know you can trust me, I love you too much to do anything to hurt you," she replied with sincere emotions.

I looked deep into her eyes and saw how genuine she was, and instantly felt bad my heart wouldn't let me fully trust her. I was always taught its M.O.B., money over bitches and I will live and die by that code. I wasn't really worried about her stealing the money because I knew she wasn't that stupid. I just needed to test her and see if I spotted any disloyalty in her heart.

"Gino?"

"What up?"

"I said I love you," she repeated to make sure I heard her the first time.

I knew she wanted me to say it back but I couldn't. I knew I loved her, but I couldn't tell her because my heart belonged to another woman. Nadia was slowly stealing my heart but before my emotions got too deep, I would have to walk away from her. I diverted my attention to my Pelle Pelle jacket hanging on the back of a chair to avoid eye contact with her.

"Aight, I'll call you in the morning when I'm on my way over here. Make sure you awake," I walked back over to her and kissed her on the forehead. "I'll holla at you later," then I walked out of the door leaving her standing there hurt.

The cool breeze of the night helped blow away the guilt I felt for toying with Nadia's emotions. I knew sooner or later I would have to break ties with her for that reason she was too innocent for a guy like me. I wanted the best for her unlike most street niggaz. But no matter the generation it seems that the good girls always fall for the bad guys, it's a repeated cycle that will never end. I hit the alarm and jumped inside of the Jeep Liberty I only drove when I didn't want to stand out in traffic.

Before I could pull off my Nextel walkie talkie chirped. I looked at the screen and seen that it was Ace.

"What's good bro?" I asked

"Aye bro, tell me why I ran into that nigga Slime and his goons up at Young's Bar-b-que about twenty minutes ago! I was expecting to start shooting, but those bitches didn't even pull steel," Ace informed me in a somewhat surprised manner.

"He ain't say shit to you?"

"Yeah, that hoe nigga told me since he can't get it in green; he'll get it in red. I didn't even respond bro, I just kept it pushing. Fuck that bitch; he ain't getting shit outta me. I should've clapped his bitch-ass when I had the drop!"

"Nawl my baby, you did the right thing. Don't even let that muthafucka wrinkle yo smooth, I'm go handle that little situation in the A.M.,"

Damn, I let it slip out! I wasn't going to tell Ace about paying Slime until after I already paid him.

"How you go handle the situation? Don't tell me you about to pay that clown all that money!" He had become angry.

"I ain't tryna hear all that rah rah shit! Yeah I'm giving his ass that little money, it's coming out of my pockets so-,"

"I don't give a fuck who paying the money, it's the fucking principles! That wanna be Nino Brown Muthafucka think everybody that walk this earth should bow down to him, and I ain't bowing down to no nigga that bleed just like me! That fuck boy ain't immortal! Ain't shit soft about me or you, but you on some Charmin type shit right now!"

"How, by saving our life and freedom, it's not about being hard or soft lil bro, it's about being smart! You can't get money and beef, how many times I'm go tell yo young ass that!?!" suddenly it was quiet on both ends of the phone.

I was beyond pissed off at my lil brother's poor decision making. It didn't take a rocket scientist to figure ain't no sense in making all this money when you can't live to enjoy it. I'm out here risking my life and freedom as it is just to live how I want to, so why would I draw extra heat to my situation by beefing with some gang bangers. It just didn't make any sense.

"Listen bro, I understand where you are coming from, and it makes a lot of sense. I respect your decision, but my heart and pride won't allow me to submit to a man I once respected and had mad love for. I thought dude was our mans."

"I feel you Ace, trust me I feel you. But a smart man draws more knowledge from his enemies than a fool from his friends. You live and you learn, but ain't no sense in living if you ain't learning. Right now we making plenty of money, to be truthful we making so much money that I'm scared to make more! You probably don't like what I'm about to do, but you'll thank me later. I'm on my way to the crib. I'll pop at you in the morning, aight."

'Aight," he responded

"Think about what I said Ace, smarten the fuck up," I hung up the phone, and stared at the screen for a brief moment. Tomorrow I planned to call Slime to set up a meeting to pay him the 1.2 million so I scrolled through my contacts to see if I still had his number stored in my phone, and stumbled across a name I didn't quite recognize.

"Who is Destiny?" I said out loud to myself. "Ohhh, Destiny!" I finally realized who she was.

Destiny was the waitress that worked at the club Zoo Bar downtown. I remembered giving her my nigga Smurf phone to keep; I can't believe I forgot to call her! It didn't make sense in wasting more time; I decided to give her a call as I finally pulled away from the curb.

"Hello," answered a soft voice.

"Is this Destiny?"

"Yes this is Destiny. How are you doing, Gino? I'm glad you finally made time to call me being as you did give me your friend phone almost two months ago."

106

"I apologize for not calling you sooner, I've been so busy working that I barely had any leisure time. By any means, that is no excuse for neglecting your feeling and I am sincerely apologetic and would love to make it up to you if you let me," she remained silent for a few seconds to digest my apology that softened her heart back up.

"When do you plan on making it up to me?" she finally asked.

"How about…right now? Where can I pick you up at?"

"You can't right now I'm at work!"

"That's even better; I'm on my way up there right now. Have a bottle of Moet on Ice for me, I'm coming alone," I told her as I made a U-turn, changing my route.

"Are you serious?" she asked giggling.

"Like T.I.," I quickly replied, merging onto the freeway.

"Like T.I.?" she asked clearly confused

"Yeah like T.I…"

"What does T.I. have to do with you being serious?"

"No, the name of T.I. first album was called-, you know what, never mind that. I'm about fifteen minutes away so be on the lookout."

'Alright, don't play me again, Gino."

"If I'm lying I'm dying," I hung up the phone.

Twenty minutes later I pulled into the parking lot of the packed club. No VIP treatment for me tonight, I was a regular nigga in the eyes of the public, and I liked it like that. I was sporting a pair of LRG jeans, black leather Pelle Pelle jacket, and a pair of white Air Force 1's. This was my laid back gear.

I slid the bouncer a Franklin to surpass the long line of searching because I was defiantly strapped. In my line of work I didn't go too many places without my pistol. I even took it to church before like I was beefing with the pastor! Like most street niggaz say, rather get caught with it then without it.

I walked into the club and the Youngbloodz smash hit "Damn!" was playing knocking through the speakers. I swerved through the thick crowd, and made my way to the VIP section where Destiny was stationed. A few tables were vacant. I spotted an empty table with a bottle of Moet sitting in an ice bucket. I sat at the unoccupied table wasting no time popping open the champagne and drinking straight from the bottle. I observed Destiny serving a table to my far left with her back towards me. I got comfortable by taking off my jacket, sitting it on the chair next to me, and then focused my attention back to Destiny. She still had that sexy allure to herself, wearing her skin tight Roca wear jeans, and a matching halter top. Her near perfect frame aroused me enough to envision myself tasting her flower. She must have felt me

108

staring at her because she turned around and gave me an intimate smile. She quickly completed her duties, hurried over to me while never breaking eye contact.

"Hey Gino!" she shrieked as I stood up and gave her a firm hug, and kiss on the cheek.

"What's good sexy, it's good to see you again," I said, inspecting her attire. After she did a full spin for me, I sat back down to nourish my taste buds.

"It's good to see you too, two months later 'Mr. I'm too busy'! Now imagine how stupid I've been looking carrying around a phone that only one person can call. I actually thought you would never call, but I still paid the freaking phone bill praying that I was wrong. And then it was a big shootout that same night you were here; I didn't know what to think! However, we can't dwell on the past, I forgive you," I took a sip of the bubbly, while I continue to stare through Destiny's pupils.

I liked Destiny a lot; she possessed this aura of loyalty and realness that attracted me to her not only physically, but also mentally. I needed a woman like her on my team that would hold me down under any circumstances. I mean, I had the love of my life at home, but Zaria wasn't what you would consider a ride or die chick. She wasn't hood at all, and didn't believe in the code of the streets being that her mother was a doctor, and she moved to a predominantly white neighborhood when she was 10 years old. I loved that innocence about my baby, but every thug needs a down ass bitch. It was a strong possibility that Destiny could be the Bonnie to my Clyde. In the midst of me deep in my thoughts, she was still standing in front of me with a curious look on her face.

"Whaaaat…? It looks like you were doing some deep thinking, what were you thinking about?" she asked placing her hands on her hips.

"I'm just overwhelmed with emotions that you actually care about a real nigga. That's a trait most females don't possess in this day and time. Me neglecting you will never happen again, trust me. No matter how much money I obtain, I can never afford to lose you. Why don't you sit down, and have a drink with me so we can get acquainted," I offered

"You know I'm working, we can't drink on the job."

"I can respect that. Quit your job so we can have a drink and get reacquainted," Destiny laughed at my idea.

"Gino you are so crazy!" she managed to say through laughter, but I didn't crack a smile.

"I was dead serious," she read my facial expressions, and recognized I wasn't joking.

"You can't be serious! I need my job Gino, I got bills to pay!"

"Baby girl, I need you to put your faith in me, okay?" after a long pause she shook her head yes. "If you put your faith in me, and remain loyal from here on out, you'll never have to stress about money for the rest of your life. I need you to trust me, can you trust me?" I asked while grabbing both of her hands, and pulling her closer. I could see the timorous in her eyes.

"Yes I can trust you, I don't know why but I feel like I can trust you."

"I want you to go get whatever belongs to you, and tell your employer you no longer work here. Then we can leave and get a bite to eat, I'll be waiting right here," I released her hands and she started to walk away but I stopped her. "Hold up baby!" I reached in my pocket and pulled out a hundred dollar bill. I handed the money to her and she pointed to the bottle of champagne I barely touched. "This is for the drinks and tell them to keep the change. Shit, they deserve it since there losing a precious employee," she gave me a half smile, and continued to walk.

She disappeared behind a door, and reappeared five minutes later with a distraught look on her face.

"You aight?" I asked once she approached me.

"I'm cool, let's just go," she replied and begin walking towards the exit.

I grabbed my jacket and followed behind her as we made our way through the crowd towards the main entrance. Once we finally made it outside, and away from the crowd, Destiny turned around to face me. I could see that her eyes started to tear up so I grabbed her to embrace her emotions.

"Gino, I don't know what it is about you but I like you a lot. I barely know you and I think I'm already deeply in love with you. I'm giving you my heart Gino, please don't break it. I'm risking everything for you right now, please don't hurt me," destiny poured her heart out to me while her head was resting on my chest, and I continued to hold her tight. She took a deep breath before continuing. "I must be a fool or have strong feeling for you to sacrifice my income. Not to mention I don't even know what you do for a living, but I don't really care. I know you might have a girlfriend and other bitches, but they don't matter to me. All I care about is being in your life and holding you down through whatever. The last two months has been the longest sixty days of my life as I waited on your call. I know you probably think I'm crazy, don't you?" she lifted her head up to look me in the eyes.

"Come on now, I don't think you're crazy. I think you've been hurt before and it's hard for you to trust niggaz, and I understand. I will never hurt you intentionally, Destiny. I'm going to make you a happy woman, I promise you that. And yes, I do have a woman whom I've been with for years. And as far as how I make money, we'll discuss that at a later time. Just know you're going to have more money than you can spend. I'm going to take good care of you little mama, and all I ask is loyalty. That's all I ask of you, and everything will fall in order. I like you a lot too, and in due time, I'm gone show you how much. But for now, let's get outta here before I end up dropping some tears and somebody see me," I joked causing her to show her beautiful smile.

I kissed her passionately on the lips for a minute straight, and I was glad to have a ride or die chick on my team. Lord knows I needed one.

Chapter Ten

Gino

I Woke up the next morning to the sound of my Nextel ringing. I came home later than usual, around two in the morning, now here it is seven in the morning and my phone disturbed my well-deserved rest. I rolled over without opening my eyes and ignored the amplifying sound.

Destiny and I ended up going to I-hop after we left the club. We ate and had a riveting conversation that lasted for hours, but only seemed like minutes. I learned a lot about her, and shared a few details about myself that kept her guessing what was in the heart of a hood nigga that rescued her from the common life, and promised her everything but the sun, stars, and the moon. It'll take time for me to fully open up my mind and heart. After we got to know each other on a mental level, it was time to part ways. I dropped her off at her sister's house that she lived with, before I dashed home to get some sleep.

Then again that plan was ruined only a few hours later due to my fucking phone continuously ringing! It better be an emergency the way they keep on calling back! I finally reached over to see who had the audacity to blow up my phone this damn early. I glanced at the screen with half open eyelids, and was surprised to see that it was my Mama who was the culprit.

"What's up Mama?" I asked with a hoarse voice.

"OH MY GOD GINO, SOMEBODY GOT AUTUMN! THEY JUST CALLED AND SAID-," she blurted out without taking a breath, so I cut her off. I was still stuck on her first sentence.

"Wait, wait, wait Mama, calm down: what do you mean they got Autumn, who got Autumn?" I asked while praying that I misunderstood everything she just said.

"I don't know who got her but they called and said they want 5 million dollars if we want her back alive! Gino, where are we going to get 5 million fucking dollars!?!   Oh my God, I pray they don't hurt my baby!" she screamed and broke down in tears.

I was in total shock, why would anybody kidnap Autumn and ask for 5 million dollars? They must think she comes from money to even request an amount of money that big. Or could it be somebody that knew me or Ace? I was in such a confused state that my hands were shaking as I tried to collect my thoughts.

"Mama I need you to calm down and listen to me. I want you to know that 5 million dollars ain't an issue; I got that all day and tomorrow. I need to know if you called the Police or not?"

"No," she whispered.

"Now tell me exactly what they said."

"I already told you what they said! The asking for 5 million dollars, and if we don't get it they going to kill her! I thought it was a joke until they put Autumn on the phone, and she was screaming and crying... then they got back on the phone and said something like, if they can't get in in green they'll get it in red, and then they hung up," I couldn't believe what she just expose to me, fuuuuuucccckk!

I had a feeling the Red Mafiya had something to do with the kidnapping! They just told Ace the exact same thing, if they can't get it in green they'll get it in red! Not paying that money to Slime got my lil sister snatched up, and ain't no telling the outcome.

"Okay Mama, whatever you do don't call the police"

"What you mean don't call the police, somebody got my damn baby!"

"I know Mama, I know! But if you call the police, and get them involved, they will kill Autumn! The money ain't a problem so don't worry about that. I just need you to calm down and listen to me so we can get her back. Please Mama, I need for you to be strong for Autumn.

116

Now listen to me, they are going to call you back, and when they do let them know you have the money, and give them my number so we can arrange a way to get them the money and get her back, I'll be over there in an hour at the most, so if they call before then, do what I asked you to do. I'm about to get everything situated then I'm on my way. I love you, please stay calm."

"I love you too, just please hurry over here," I hung up the phone and instantly called Slime number but got no answer.

I couldn't believe that Slime would stoop this low as if we don't know each other at all! I highly doubt he would hurt Autumn as long as I didn't test his manhood and just pay the ransom, but then again everything was unpredictable because I never thought he would pull a stunt like this. If we would've been paid that nigga this shit would've never happened! If my Mama found out that we were the reason behind Autumn getting kidnapped, she would never forgive us.

I looked over to the other side of the bed and finally realized that Zaria was missing. I went to the bathroom only to find it empty, so I walked to the living room where I found her sleeping on the sofa.

"Zaria...Zaria," I shook her shoulder as I called her.

"What?" she replied with an attitude?

"Why are you sleeping on the fucking couch?"

"Because I refuse to sleep in a bed with you smelling like another bitch cheap perfume," she rolled her eyes and rolled over like she was going back to sleep.

Instead of arguing, I just walked back to the bedroom because I had way more important shit to worry about then Zaria being mad at me. As I sat on the bed to get my plan together, I could hear Zaria's footsteps thundering towards me. She burst through the door and towered over me with her hands resting on her hips.

"So you just go walk away like fuck how I feel, huh!"

"Not right now Zaria, I ain't got time for yo bullshit," I replied as calmly as I could while covering my face with my hands.

"What the fuck you mean you ain't got time, Gino? You got time to be out in them streets with some bitch at two in the morning, but you ain't got time for your woman? I'm so tired-"

"I said I don't have time for no bullshit so go sit yo ass down somewhere! I got some serious shit I need to take care of so shut the fuck up with all that dramatic shit!"

"So what's more important than our relationship right now, Giovanni? What's so important that we can't talk?"

"Somebody kidnapped Autumn," I somberly responded.

"What...? Somebody kidnapped Autumn?" she asked in shock.

"Yeah, somebody got my lil sister."

"Who got her?"

"That's what I'm tryna figure out right now, and I don't want to talk about it. I'm just focused on getting her back," I knew who had my sister, but its certain shit you didn't discuss with your woman, especially when it was concerning the streets. Won't catch me pillow talking with no bitch!

"I'm sorry baby, I'm so sorry!" She leaned down and gave me a hug, and her tears landed on my cheek.

"Ssh…don't worry about it, everything will be alright. We gone get her back, and I put that on my life," I meant every word.

After I calmed Zaria down, I called Ace and told him to gather up 3.8 million immediately and meet me at Mama's house. He wanted an explanation but I told him I'll explain once he got there. After I talked to him, I went straight over to Nadia's apartment to pick up the 1.2 million I left over there last night.

Seventeen hours later me, Ace, and my boy Lo-Lo were sitting at my Mama's dining room table patiently waiting on the call from the kidnappers. It was almost three in the morning, and we still haven't received a call about Autumn's well-being. I even tried to call Slime several times but he never answered. The waiting process was eating at my nerves, trying not to think about the worst possible outcome. I was silently praying that she was ok, which, was all I could do.

Sitting at the table restless, flicking a butterfly knife open and close, Ace was sitting at the opposite end sipping on a fifth of Remy Martin VSOP, and Lo-Lo was seated next to me with his head resting on the table and his finger tapping the table in a rhythm. I had called Lo-Lo for reinforcement just in case things got out of hand.

Pleading with my Mama to go upstairs and get some rest, she finally took my advice an hour ago instead of stressing herself out by thinking the worst. She was so accustomed to seeing the outcome of being kidnapped in the movies, and on T.V. that she made up her mind that she may never see her only daughter alive again. Wishing like hell she didn't have to go through this whole ordeal, because truth be told, she was hurting more than I could ever hurt even though she was my sister.

Sitting at the table secretly furious with Ace's poor decision making skills, not only was he sitting here getting drunk at a time he's supposed to be focused, however, I felt that he was the main reason that we were going through all this turmoil. If only he would've put his pride aside and paid the Red Mafiya, Autumn would be sound asleep in her own room right now. Just thinking about it got my blood boiling; I refused to bite my tongue any longer. I sat up straight in my chair, and placed the butterfly knife on the table in front of me.

"So…you just gone sit there and fog up your mind drinking that bullshit?" I asked staring directly at Ace.

He put the bottle up to his lips and took another swig of the Remy, and lowered it to the table with his hand still wrapped around it. He diverted his eyes to mine and cleared his throat.

"You got a problem with the way I deal with my frustrations?" he asked with a hint of aggression.

"Nawl, I can't tell you how to deal with anything, you're a grown ass man, right? But I do have a problem with the way you handle situations that put our own family at risk. If you-"

"You are so fucking predictable! I know what you've been sitting over there thinking this whole time. Let me guess, you was just about to say if I had been paid Slime then this would've never happened, right?"

"At least you see your faults, lil bro."

"Fuck YOU NIGGA, AND FUCK SLIME TOO!" screamed Ace causing Lo-Lo to finally lift his head. "If you weren't so scary then we could've been murked Slime and whoever else got in our way!"

'Oh you mean murk Slime, and then the 50,000 FUCKING SOLDIERS THAT'S HERE IN DETROIT!" I yelled sarcastically but truthfully.

"I don't give a fuck how many niggaz it is, I'm ready to ride!"

"You ain't ready for shit, you ain't cut like that! I shot back and looked him dead in the eyes when I said it.

"Gino, fuck you! Don't blame me, blame your damn self!" I could see the tears building in his eyes. "The real problem is you think you better than me! You think you smarter than me, you underestimate me like I can't think, but I got this shit popping!"

"I don't know where you got that idea from, but you can dead it!"

"Why in the hell are y'all yelling in the house at three in the morning?!" Mama screamed catching us all by surprise.

"Nothing Mama, we're sorry for waking you up. Go ahead and go back to bed," I said as I stood up, and put my arm around her shoulder trying to lead her back to the stairs.

"It must not be okay the way y'all down here yelling, now tell me what's going on! Is Autumn okay?" she asked, but before any of us could say anything the house phone begin to ring.

Everybody directed their attention to the phone, and I was hoping that it was the call we were waiting for. I walked over to where I was sitting and glanced down at the phone as it was on its second ring. Before the third ring chimed, I picked up the receiver.

122

"Who this?" I asked

"I take it this is either Gino or Ace? I don't need you to talk B, just grab some paper and a pen, and listen," he instructed me and I snapped my finger and pointed at the pen at the other end of the table. Lo-Lo grabbed the pen for me, and I listened carefully. "Now listen, we both know 5 million in cash is the ticket, nothing less. I need you to bring the money to Prairie Street and Florence, right off of Puritan Avenue. You got one hour to deliver the money to that location. Someone will be there to collect the money, so if you try some slick shit, then it's off with her head. After we collect the money and count it, I will tell you where to pick this bitch up at," just as I was about to give him my cell phone number he hung up. How the fuck he gone tell me where to pick up Autumn if he don't have my number?

Ace, Mama, and Lo-Lo stood there staring at me waiting for me to say something. I picked up the butterfly knife and put it in my pocket, grabbed my Mac 90 off the table and switched back to load a bullet in the chamber.

"Lo-Lo, I want you to ride with me- you know what, scratch that, Ace ride with me. Lo-Lo you follow behind us with the money, we on our way to the Westside."

I was driving in the Jeep with Ace, and Lo-Lo followed closely in his low-key Ford Contour with the 5 million dollars. We were riding up

Puritan Avenue coming down Livernois, driving a little bit over the speed limit. We had been riding for over twenty-five minutes, and we haven't said one word to each other. The way we truly felt about each other was exposed, and both of us didn't like it. But it was always said that a pretty lie looked better than the ugly truth. Everything was destined to smooth over once we got Autumn back, but if we didn't I knew our relationship was beyond repair.

I finally made it to Prairie Street, and made a sharp right. I drove all the way down the block until I reached the dead end which was Florence Street, and then I made a left. The street was dark due to the streetlights being shot out; it was only illuminated by the headlights on my Jeep. I checked my rearview mirror to make sure Lo-Lo was still behind us before climbing out of the Jeep.

Ace and I walked back to Lo-Lo car where I grabbed the bags of money out of his trunk. I instructed both of them to stay alert and ready to shoot, and then strolled towards the dead-end by my lonesome so there were no misunderstandings with the opposition, and stood there for approximately two minutes before my phone unexpectedly rung.

"What's next?" I asked not bothering to think about how he got my number.

"Drop the bag right there, and retreat back to your car then drive off. Don't worry, you will get your sister back alive and that's on my set.

124

After we thumb through this paper we go hit you back, so keep your phone on, it'll be about thirty minutes," and then he hung up. I dropped the bags of money and walked back to the Jeep where Lo-Lo and Ace were still standing silently.

"Ace, get in the car with Lo-Lo, I'll follow y'all to the Gas- Station on Livernois Avenue," we got in our cars and then pulled off, leaving 5 million dollars in cash without taking Autumn with us. It's just a chance I had to take in order to get my little sister back. I wasn't in the position to negotiate shit!

After we met up at the Gas-Station, we agreed to wait on that important call at the Coney Island on W. McNichol's and Livernois. We all sat in silence as I sipped on some orange juice, while the cashier and a couple of the employees continued to glance at us as if they could tell something was wrong.

It seemed like I prayed every ten seconds that we would get Autumn back safely because if it was one scratch on her, it was defiantly going to be a bloody summer! She didn't deserve to be in this predicament at all, but it wasn't any rules to this game I played no matter how many times we tried to implement some. As much as I tried to shift the blame on Ace, deep down I felt it was my fault as much as it was his. If only I would've delivered Slime that money a day sooner…Finally the phone rung after what seemed like a decade, I immediately flipped the phone open.

125

"Talk to me…"

"This Gino right?"

"Yeah, this him," I replied.

"Good, pay close attention because I'm only going to say this once. Any retaliation will result in the death of your whole immediate family courtesy of the Red Mafiya. Then after they are dead, you and Ace will be next. Let this be a lesson learned for fucking with my set. You can pick you sister up in yo girl old backyard on Hartwell, the keys are in the glove compartment," and he hung up for the last time.

I hurriedly jumped to my feet and ran out of the Coney Island with Ace and Lo-Lo in quick pursuit! I started the engine, and slammed the gear in drive.

"Where she at?" asked a frantic Ace.

"On Hartwell at Zaria's old house."

I drove into traffic, and got to Hartwell in less than five minutes flat while Lo-Lo followed closely. I pulled in the driveway and could see Autumn's 2004 Infiniti G37K in the backyard. I put the Jeep in park, grabbed my Mack 90, and slipped out of the car. We all walked slowly towards her car while scanning the scene to make sure it wasn't an ambush. I made it to the driver's side door and looked in the window to

126

find it empty. I opened the unlocked door, and suddenly heard a muffled noise coming from the trunk.

"Gino, she in the trunk! We need to get this fucking trunk open!" Ace screamed as he begins to panic.

I got in the car and popped open the glove compartment where I was told the keys were, sprinted back to the trunk as I pushed the trunk button on the keypad to find Autumn tied up at the wrist and ankles, with grey duct tape covering her mouth. When I saw the blood stains on her pants, and shirt I almost broke down. Ace and Lo-Lo shoved me to the side, and lifted her out of the trunk as gently as they could. I grabbed the butterfly knife out of my pocket and followed behind Ace as him and Lo-Lo laid her on the backseat. When they moved out of the way I eased the tape off her mouth.

"GINO! OH MY GOD GINO" cried Autumn.

"It's okay baby, we got you back now. Don't worry baby girl everything gone be alright. Be still so I can cut you loose. "I tried to calm her down while I cut her wrist and ankles loose. She then leaped up and hugged me as tightly as she could and continued to sob.

"Ssh, stop crying Autumn…you safe now," I assured her.

I was…so scared: He raped me!" she wailed, and my heart dropped to the bottom of my stomach.

"Who raped you!?! Do you know who it was?" asked Ace.

"I couldn't see, I was blindfolded the whole time… I was so scared. I thought I was going to die!" I had a single tear streaming down my face, and then looked over at Ace and his face was stained with tears.

"Come on Autumn, let's get you home," I picked up my little sister and carried her to the Jeep, laying her on the backseat. After making sure she was comfortable, I got behind the wheel and took off to my condo. I chose not to take her to my Mama house in such a disheveled state; she would have fainted at the sight of Autumn's current condition.

I have never felt so much rage in my entire life, and I made vow to myself that somebody would pay. Slime did the unthinkable by fucking with my family, and he had to die for it. If that meant I had to die in the process, I'll die with the sweet taste of revenge on my tongue.

Chapter Eleven

Ace

I Couldn't believe Gino had the nerves to say it was my fault that Autumn got kidnapped! Although it's been two weeks since we got her back, I still couldn't let go how he tried to play me like a straight bitch! That boy got me all fucked up," I mumbled to myself sitting alone in my living room watching Sportscenter. I reached into the ashtray that sat on the grey and white marble table, and grabbed the already rolled Purple Haze blunt. I put fire to the blunt and sat back on the black leather sectional sofa, and continued to let my mind wonder.

This muthafucka come home and think he running shit when I'm the one who put us on our feet, and moved Mama outta the hood. Ever since he hit that lick on Mook for that money and those bricks of Blow, he has been acting like he the H.N.I.C (Head Nigga In Charge)! He lucky he my brother or I would've been put some holes in his bitch-ass for fronting on me in front of his bitch-ass homeboy Lo-Lo! Go tell me I'm not cut like that, nigga you ain't cut like that! It seems like he more loyal to Lo-Lo than he is to me. That bitch Lo-Lo wasn't there when he was doing that bid, I was! He wasn't putting money on his books every week like clockwork, I was! He wasn't making sure his visits were popping every week, muthafucka I was! But yet and still he treated that nigga like a brother, and treated me like a distant relative. Man... fuck him!

Just as I was about to take another pull of the blunt, my Nextel started ringing. I looked at the screen to see who it was calling, and couldn't stop myself from smiling before I answered it.

"What up doe lil mama?" I was just thinking about yo sexy ass," I lied

"Is that right? Well, I hope you don't have any company because I'm a few minutes away."

"Nawl ain't nobody else here with me. Just get yo freaky ass over here so I can relieve some frustrations out on that pussy, hurry up!"

"You just make sure your door is unlocked, silly," she giggled before she hung up.

I jumped to my feet, and unlocked the front door before dashing upstairs to my bedroom to stash the 250 bands of hundred dollar bills just lying across the bed. Just as I got all the money in the floor safe in my walk-in closet, I heard the house alarm beep from the front door being opened.

"Ace!" the familiar female voice called out.

"I'm up here!" I yelled back, and then went to my bathroom to dispose the small blunt I had been smoking. After I flushed it, I took off my shirt as I entered the bedroom and dropped it at the end of the bed just as she came in the room waving through the clouds of Haze smoke.

"Oh my God, you got the whole house smoky, boy!"

"That's the only way I can remain sane. Come here, you looking good today," she walked over to me and planted a wet kiss on my lips.

"You like my outfit?" She asked as she did a full three-sixty.

"Yeah I do… now take it off," I demanded, and she immediately complied with my instructions.

I sat on the edge of the bed and watched her little strip tease, her body flawless as the first day I seen her naked, and I couldn't get enough of her radiant beauty. Once she stripped down to her black lace thong and bra, I slipped out of my Evisu jeans and Polo boxers, my dick harder than a jawbreaker. I pulled her closer to me and proceeded to kiss her stomach and lick her navel. I reached around her waist to slide my hand between her ass cheeks to spread them apart; I knew her pussy walls were pulsating and extra moist from the anal penetration.

I stopped kissing her stomach then looked up, her eyes were closed and her head was leaned back enjoying the finger fucking. I pulled my finger out and wiped it on the bed sheets before she looked down at me with slanted eyes. Grabbing her by her shoulders and guiding her down to her knees, she knew exactly what I was hinting at. She took my dick in her hand, and stroked it a few times before kissing around the head with precision. She teased me for a few minutes before actually putting it in her mouth and sucking it like a vacuum sucked dirt! It didn't take long for me to reach my nut, releasing in her mouth without warning but she made sure to swallow every last drop just like I taught her to.

"Now it's my turn," she replied while standing up to take off her thong and bra.

"Yes it is. How long do I have before you have to leave me?" I asked knowing her man might be blowing up her phone soon.

"However long you want me to stay."

"You sure your man won't be looking for you?"

"No he won't, and he will never think I'm here. Gino is at y'all Mama House right now anyway. When did you start worrying about him, you scared he might pop up?" she asked climbing up on the bed and laying down spread eagle.

"Number one. I ain't scared of shit so let's get that clear. Number two, you the one that should be worried about him catching us, not me," I said stating the facts.

"Why should I be the one worried and not you?"

"Because I know my brother like I know the back of my hands. He might be mad at me for a minute if he found out about us, but he might try to kill you, Zaria," I answered honestly.

"Would you try to protect me if he tried to hurt me?" she asked with a look of fear in her eyes, and I felt kind of bad for continuously fucking with her behind Gino back, but I didn't put a gun up to her head and force her to do anything.

I started fucking Zaria almost two years ago, and in my mind it wasn't my fault because she initiated our first sexual encounter. I came to her house one day to drop off a couple thousand and was greeted by her at the door wearing a bright smile, and her tailor made birthday suit!

From that day forward, I was having sex with her at least four times a week. I knew how disloyal it was to be fucking my brothers' main bitch on the low, but I felt like I was addicted to her sexual prowess. Every time we had sex it was always better than the last time, and that kept me feenin for more. The thought of us getting caught always crossed my mind, but that didn't stop me from getting my fix. Gino probably would stop fucking with me, but I know for a fact the he loved Zaria so much, he would probably kill her. Truthfully, if he tried to hurt her in any way, I wouldn't move a muscle to try and defend her. But I had to tell her what she wanted to hear.

"You know I got you baby, I wouldn't let that nigga lay a finger on you," I lied, but Zaria smile let me know she was content with my response.

"Good. Now come eat this pussy," and without hesitation I complied with her instructions.

******

I pulled up in my S-550 Benz on bloom street right off 7 Mile Road, to one of our houses that we stashed weight at. I parked all the way in the backyard before I chirped Mitch who was babysitting the house, and told him to unlock the side door burglar gate for me. I periodically checked on all the weight and stash houses to make sure everything was ran right, and today I was moving from house to house since I was ducked off for so long. Sometimes you had to show your face to your workers to let them know you were still on top of your game, and weren't slacking on your job.

Mitch was in charge of this specific house, and seldom left it unless he was tending to business elsewhere. My job was to make sure the rules were enforced at all times, and the number one rule was: Nobody was allowed inside the houses besides Me, Gino, and the person in charge of that particular house. That meant no bitches, homies, family, not even yo fucking Mama! The number two rule was: No stealing. Nothing should come up missing without a valid reason why. The number three rule was: No using any drugs while at the house. We wanted every worker sober and on high alert at all times: No matter how much people debate it, it's a scientific fact that illegal drugs altered your way of thinking. So in order to be in charge of any of our houses you had to have a clear mind. Needless to say if any of these rules were violated, the consequence will be nothing less than death. Plain and simple.

I hopped out of my spaceship, and wobbled my way to the side door because Zaria drained me for all the little energy I had. The gate was unlocked and Mitch was standing in the threshold with a fully loaded AR-15 equipped with a hundred round drum.

"What's good my baby?" I stepped inside the house to the smell of stale air, and leftover food from the neighborhood Coney Island.

I strolled into the living room and a PlayStation 2 was resting on the floor beneath a 52 inch Plasma TV bolted to the wall. Mitch retreated back to the Lazy boy and picked up the game controller.

"Ain't shit up with me, just playing this Madden 04. You wanna get yo ass whupped in this shit?" Challenged Mitch.

"Do I look like I came here to play a fucking video game?"

"You sound just like yo uptight brother with all that rah rah shit. He came through here earlier mad at the world, and taking it out on everybody but the source of the problem," replied Mitch shaking his head while I took a seat on the couch and propped my feet on the table.

"Oh yeah, what he come through for, inventory?"

"Fuck yeah, and he ain't even do that right! I don't like his Wannabe Godfather muthafucka whole aura, Ace. I know that's yo brother and all, but I can't rock with that nigga. Let's get this clear, I fuck with you, I don't even know that lame and he trying to tell me what to do. I get the vibe he don't like me and the feeling is mutual.

"Just be cool, he probably still mad about the Autumn situation."

"Real talk, if I was you I wouldn't be giving him access to all my spots and money. I can tell y'all ain't close like me and Mel is, but I also see that comes from him thinking he's the boss of you. The nigga coming over here double checking how you handle business ain't no real shit to me. He acts like he doesn't trust you or something."

Everything Mitch was saying had some truth to it and I felt the exact same way, he seemed to dictate every thought or move I made since he came home. Once upon a time I thought we were real close, but it seems that time and money has changed that. The beef with the Red Mafiya hindered our once air tight relationship, and if Gino let them Red bitches come between us then so be it.

"But seriously Ace, I know you ain't turned soft like that," he stated and I instantly snapped.

"Who the fuck you think you talking too? You need to watch yo muthafucking mouth little ass boy before I put these hands and feet on you!" he struck a nerve when he mentioned my name and soft in the same category. "You play your position and don't worry about how me and my brother run shit as long as you get paid! Know your role playboy before you open yo mouth," I reminded him as I got up from the couch to inspect the house and product.

The place was a two story brick house with a basement, but Mitch was only allowed on the main floor where we kept a certain amount of bricks stored for easy access. We always locked the door to the basement even though it was completely empty. Gino and I were the only ones allowed on the top floor also, that's where the major weight was held.

I checked the basement and the main floor to make sure everything was secure and intact. Then I went to the kitchen where the bricks Mitch had access to were stashed in the oven, and it was only six bricks when it was supposed to be ten at all times. I went back to the living room to confront Mitch.

"You said Gino came through, why you only got six bricks in the stash?"

"I told his ass the policy, and all he said was 'You'll be alright', so I left it alone," he answered nonchalant.

I didn't even respond, I went upstairs where I was greeted by a locked Iron Gate and steel door. After unlocking the gate and door, I went to the oak wood desk that was occupied by a new computer no one ever used, and a fax machine that wasn't even plugged in. I picked up the inventory sheet, and then counted the bricks that were stacked on the bookshelf. Once I completed the survey, I grabbed four of the bricks, and then changed the quantity on the sheet and put today's date and time. I made sure everything was in order, secured the door and gate, and went back downstairs to find Mitch still in the same position playing the video game.

"Here, put these up with the rest of them. I'm sliding up outta here, make sure you call me before you leave," I instructed him, tossing the birds on the couch next to him.

'Aight, I'll pop at you later. You got something shaking tonight," asked Mitch, rising to his feet grabbing the bricks.

"I ain't got shit up, you tryna ride downtown tonight?"

"I don't know yet I still gotta holla at Mel."

"Aight let me know what y'all gone do so I can go cop me something to fuck."

"Cool, I'll let you know before the sun goes down."

I walked back out into the sweltering heat, and damn near ran to get in my car to turn on the AC. As soon as I hit the alarm my phone started ringing.

"What up," I answered

"OH MY GOD, SHE'S DEAD!!"

Chapter Twelve

Autumn

It had been three weeks since I was set free by my abductors, but I still feel as if I was being held captive mentally. I never thought or imagined me being a victim of rape; I always said that only the sexually provocative became targets but how wrong was I. I was traumatized to the degree that I hardly wanted to do anything or go anywhere. My Mama and brothers checked on me on a regular basis and tried everything to make me feel better, but I was terrified to go anywhere and be around a bunch of strangers.

A few days after I was released I was somewhat stable enough to discuss the events that took place with my brothers and mother, and we all cried together as I told them everything that transpired. I was coming out of the Eastland Mall with my hands full of shopping bags, and once I reached the trunk of my car a shadow appeared behind me but before I could turn around I was roughly grabbed and stuffed into my own trunk. It seemed like I was in the trunk for hours before the car came to an abrupt halt and I prayed who was ever behind the wheel didn't kill me. When the trunk finally opened the light from the sky was so bright I was temporarily blinded, and before my eyes could adjust to the light my head was covered by what appeared to be a pillow case. I was then lifted out of the trunk by both of my arms and placed on my feet to walk on my own. A deep voice told me to remain calm and follow directions and I would be back home soon.

I was escorted inside a house and down a flight of stairs where the temperature changed to damp and cool which gave me the assumption that it was a basement. I was then led into an isolated room where the bag was taken off my head but to my surprise I still couldn't see because the room was pitch black. A door was closed and then locked and I was left in the small room with no windows or light fixture. After standing for a while I took a seat on the cold concrete floor and curled up into a ball and silently cried. After so many hours somebody came back and handed me two sandwiches and a bottle of water that I refused to eat or drink, but I didn't protest for too long because a gun was pressed against my temple and I was told to eat and drink up.

After scoffing down the sandwich and water the kidnapper left and I leaned up against the concrete wall wondering why I was picked out of all the women in the world. Just as I was thinking about how I could escape, the door was swung open so hard that it hit the wall with a thud. I was then grabbed by my throat and told to take all my clothes off. I put up a fight before I felt the cold steel of his gun pressed against my head and I immediately complied.

I pulled my pants and panties down while weeping, my pride slowly evaporating into thin air. He forced me to the ground, and then mounted me. He violated me for at least twenty minutes and I laid there limp, crying the whole time. He took whatever innocence I had left and destroyed it for an unknown reason and I felt like dying. The thought was so hard to shake that I found myself thinking about the gruesome nightmare every single hour of every single day. A couple weeks ago I went to the health clinic with Gino to get myself tested for any diseases just to be on the safe side, and the doctor said it should take up to a week for the results. Right now I was lying across my bed still in shock at the unexpected turn my life took. I reached over to my nightstand, grabbed a sheet of paper, and read it carefully for the thousandth time.

"Positive," I mumbled to myself in bewilderment.

It seemed that my eyes could never run dry because all I did was constantly cry. I knew crying couldn't help or change my situation, but I couldn't control my emotions. The fresh tears rolled down my face and landed down my pillow leaving a salty wet spot.

I sat up in bed and blew my nose with an already soiled piece of tissue. I could smell my own funky body odor, the smell of not washing up for the third straight day but I didn't care. I didn't care about anything, not even living. I read the sheet of paper again and tear streamed down profusely.

"Positive," I whispered to myself again.

I stood up and slowly dragged my feet to my window and peeked out of the blinds. A number of kids were outside on the sunny day riding their bikes and having pure fun. A group of little girls were jump roping and singing a nursery rhyme in unison. What I wouldn't give to be that age again, and to be that at peace. I looked up at the sky and asked God why, then quickly apologized for questioning my higher power. I said a silent prayer, and I asked for peace and forgiveness because I was a lost soul…a lost cause.

I hesitantly walked over to my closet and opened the door, squatted down in a comfortable position and reached into one of many shoe boxes, and pulled out a chrome .380 handgun. I retreated back to my bed and took a seat at the foot of it, and cradled the gun in both of my hands.

"I'm so sorry…," I said to no one in particular.

"I was emotionally drained and physically exhausted. The mental torture took a toll on me and I couldn't get a grip on reality. I checked the chamber to make sure it was loaded, and then placed the pistol to my right temple. I mouthed another silent prayer and suddenly my bedroom door was opened.

"Autumn you want to-," my mother was frozen once she spotted what was taking place.

BOOM!!

Autumn's lifeless body fell to the floor as her mother stood in the doorway with her mouth wide open in dismay.

Chapter Thirteen

Gino

Missing someone isn't about how long it's been since you've seen them last or how long it's been since you've last talked. It's about that very moment when you're doing something and you wish that they were right there with you.

I read that quote in some book while I was in prison, and I couldn't fathom on how accurate it could be until I lost someone dear to me.

"We are gathered here today to celebrate the life of the beautiful and beloved, Autumn Essence Jones, who made the transition to the afterlife on July 12, 2003," Pastor Thomas began to preach, but I tuned him out.

I was sitting on the first pew with my immediate family at my little sister's funeral. My Mama was sitting next to me with a distant look in her eyes and a stained face of tears. Ace was on the other side of me starring at his hands that was planted on his lap, and I could see his eyes were like dark clouds ready to release his rain of tears. I just sat there, my face expressionless, my tear ducts had dried up, I had no more cry in me.

144

It's been five days since Autumn committed suicide and I still couldn't believe she was really gone and not coming back. She left no note or explanation and that left us all somewhat puzzled until the police found the results of her HIV test which came back positive. For the past five days all I could do was sit in my condo and try to drink my pain away. My heart was beyond broken, the pain sometimes so unbearable that I actually thought about taking my own life. But my yearning for vengeance is what gave me the breath to live another day. These niggaz took my sister away from me and somebody had to pay, and that somebody will be Slime! I lay in the bed all day thinking of strategies to kill Slime. Sure it'll be risky and I might get killed when it's all said and done, but I was willing to take that sacrifice for the sake of Autumn. I felt guilty for her death and killing Slime won't buy me happiness but it's a damn good down payment.

I was so caught up in my own web of thoughts of retaliation that I didn't notice the Pastor sermon was coming to a close. I turned around to the back of the packed church and spotted Destiny standing near the exit. She made eye contact with me and gave me an empathy smile along with a quick wave.

After turning back around I looked over at Zaria who was consoling my Mama, and was glad she was there for me and my family at a time like this. The Pastor requested for everybody to stand while he said his final prayer, and I couldn't tell you what everybody else prayed for but I prayed for insight and strength. Insight to know if revenge was worth it, and strength to execute my revenge no matter the insight.

After the eulogy it seemed that everybody in the whole church crowed around us to pay their respects, but I made my way through the crowd after hugging my Mama. I was walking towards the exit in search of Destiny, and spotted her standing on the sidewalk in front of the church. I slowly approached her and once I reached her she gave me a short but poignant hug.

"I'm sorry for your loss Gino, your sister was a beautiful woman," said Destiny with genuine emotion as she held eye contact.

"You shouldn't be sorry, but I appreciate your condolence. What's up with you?"

"Nothing much, you know I had to come and pay my respects. I think I'll leave before somebody sees us and start assuming."

"Don't say it like that; you can stay as long as you want to. I don't care who see us standing here together," Destiny smiled at my remark and I . could feel my heart warm up from this cold day.

I was defiantly feeling Destiny, the way she carried herself as a loyal woman left an imprint on my heart. When we finally got Autumn back I started spending a lot more time with her to get my mind off my sisters suffering. I moved her out of her house and bought her a four bedroom newly renovated brick house in Farmington Hills, and paid cash for her

BLOOD B4 BETRAYAL

2004 Mercedes Benz CLK fresh off the assembly line. I purchased her all new furniture and appliances to make sure her new home was well furnished, and she took pride in making sure the decorations looked as if it was a job of a professional.

I had a plan for Destiny rather she noticed it or not, I was in the process of molding her into a woman that every real nigga wish he had on his team. We recently discussed her obtaining a Real Estate License so she can start a lucrative career in a wealthy field. The first step to reaching her goal was she had to enroll in night classes that wouldn't take that long to complete. Although we just met over a month ago, I was connected to her in a way I never felt before, not even with Zaria. I felt compelled to provide for her and give her a better life and opportunity, so that's exactly what I was doing.

"Aww, aren't you the sweetest! I appreciate the gesture but I know my position, Gino. The last thing I would want is to get into a confrontation at your sisters funeral with your girl-"and as if on cue out of my periphery I spotted Zaria coming down the stairs, and headed in our direction.

Destiny sensed something was wrong because she instantly stopped talking and followed my line of sight.

"Hey baby," greeted Zaria as she gave me a quick kiss on the lips.

"I was just looking for you," she turned around and looked at Destiny.

"I'm sorry where are my manners, I'm Zaria and you are?"

"Hello I'm Destiny, a friend of Autumn," she replied, extending her hand and shaking Zaria's.

"Oh Okay, its nice meeting you Destiny, I'm glad you could make the funeral. How long were you two friends?"

"We both met our freshman year at Baker College when we were 18 years old. She was one of my closest friends, and I was just telling Gino about the last time I seen her."

"Don't let me interrupt you guy's conversation, I just stop to introduce myself. I'm going back into the church with Mama baby; it's nice to meet you, Destiny."

"You to Zaria," Destiny responded, and then Zaria begins to walk away hesitantly.

"You just won the Oscar for Best Actress!" I joked once Zaria was out of ear shot.

We both burst out laughing causing Zaria to glance back at us out of curiosity and insecurity.

"But seriously, I appreciate that. That right there lets me know that you're a down chick no matter what. Now in order to keep it that way we can never fall in love with each other."

"It's a little bit too late for that," replies Destiny.

"Yeah I know," was all I could say.

I gave Destiny a hug and watched her walk to her Benz and drive off. Just as I was turning to leave I heard a voice call my name.

"Mr. Irby!" A frail looking white guy in a navy blue suite screamed my name again as he crossed the busy street.

I was on high alert because his face was unfamiliar, but I noticed he had a dozen white Roses in his hand and an envelope in the other. Once he reached me he held out the Roses and envelope for me to grab.

"Mr. Irby, hello how are you? These are for you, sorry for your lost. My condolence goes out to your family," and before I could ask him who he was, he was gone as quick as he came.

I starred at the departing back of the mysterious man as he disappeared around a corner. I finally opened the envelope and inside was a black card with red lettering. I opened up the card and it read,

'My condolence goes out to you and the family my nigga, if anything is needed I'm only a call away.'

-Sincerely, OG Slime

I can't believe this bitch-ass nigga had the nerves to send some fucking roses and a card! Slime knew how to get under my skin, and I plan to make him suffer for his deliberate arrogance. That hoe nigga got it coming and that's on everything! I dropped the roses on the pavement in front of the church, and went back to join my family.

******

"Everybody should already know why we're here today. I appreciate the whole team paying their respect at the funeral that meant a lot to a nigga. I called this meeting and invited you specifically because you gained the trust or loyalty of either me or my brother," I looked at each individual carefully, and wondered who was the flaw in our circle. Since no one in particular showed me, then I would have to put my trust in each of them and hope for nothing but honor.

After the burial service I called a meeting and invited only the key players in our circle which consisted of: Lo-Lo, Mitch and Mel, Murda, and my boy Smurf. We were in the back room of the pool hall Lo-Lo owned called Billiards on Woodward Ave. Although we could hear the music and conversations being held outside of the office, I felt that this was the most secure place to hold a meeting of this magnitude.

The spacious office was well furnished with a marble and leather decor, marble desk, bar, and tables, leather chairs, bar stools, and curtains. The office was located on the second floor where eight pool tables occupied the open space behind the office double doors. In the middle of the office floor set a marble conference table with eight leather chairs surrounding it, and that's where we all were seated.

"And I pray every day that none of you will betray that trust between us. Everybody that's present is making plenty money and got plenty more to make, but none of that shit means anything if we don't get our well-deserved respect. And as of now, the Red Mafiya don't respect us. These Red pussies I had to pause for a few seconds to let the agony in my heart pass over. "…took my baby girl away with no remorse, and I can't let that slide. And if y'all were in our position, you wouldn't let that slide either."

"Listen Gino, you my mans and I'll ride with you until the end with no question. I just want you to think about the risk we are about to take, and if you still want to go at these niggaz, let's go get it," said Smurf.

"I understand what you're hinting at my nigga, but I don't give a fuck about how much of a risk I'm taking, that's how serious I am. My main purpose is to kill Slime; I don't want anybody but that bitch. Whoever tries to stop my purpose will be dealt with accordingly. None of you will be on the front line; I just want to know if I call on you to squeeze those triggers will you be front and center?"

"What you mean not going to be on the front line?" asked Mel.

"I'm glad you asked that. As you know I already got a team of trigger happy niggaz that love killing almost as much as they love money. My Flint niggaz gone take care of all the heavy work for us, and hopefully they deliver Slime to me on a platter. They will be taking care of all the footwork, so in the meantime we're going to continue to stack our paper and stay below the radar. Once again, I just need to know if the time presents itself and I need you, will you be there for me." Before anybody could answer that question we were disturbed by a knock at the door, and then Lo-Lo's manager of the pool hall Steve stuck his head in the room.

"Sorry to interrupt you gentlemen, but its a few gentlemen here that request to see you," said a clearly nervous Steve.

"Who the fuck is it Steve?" asked Lo-Lo.

We all found out when several men dressed in all black bombarded their way into the office! We all stood, pulled out our pistols, and aimed them at the unwanted guests. They responded by pulling out their own weapons and pointing them at us with a blank expression and steady hand. The men dressed in all black stepped aside and in strolled the man I hated with all my heart. He stopped in front of his militia of men, and gave a sly smirk.

"Whoa, whoa fellas! What's the cause of all this hostility, don't we see enough of this black of black violence?" joked Slime.

He was dressed in a jogging suit with the word R.E.D in black letters across the chest of his red hoodie, R.E.D meant: Real Enemies Die. My first instinct was to fill his body up with every bullet in my clip, but we all would have probably died if I did that. My adrenaline was in

152

overdrive and I could taste blood, but I kept my composure and put on my poker face.

"I guess you in the mood to let your nuts hang, huh?" I managed to say through my grimace facial expression.

"I meant no disrespect, Gino. You know I got mad love for you and your peoples, I just drop by to say what up and see how you were doing."

"So your way of saying what up is barging up in my man's establishment, and pointing guns at my peoples?" I asked nodding at his goons.

"Come on fam! Your people aren't saints themselves, look at em," Slime smiled at the scene.

"So could you tell your foot soldiers to lower their guns?"

"Probably…not," replied Slime.

"Okay, let's cut the small talk, whatever you got to say, say it and then get the fuck outta here."

"Wow, I see prison made you a real tuff guy! I bet you caught all type of serious tickets like…Threaten Behavior and Insolence!" a few of his goons laughed at his sarcastic comment, and my blood pressure became higher than before.

Slime began to walk around the office as if he owed the place, and then took a seat on the bar stool before he continued to talk.

"But seriously, I just came here to talk with you and your brother to see what was on y'all mind being that you just buried your little sister. I sincerely apologize for your lost; you know she was like a sister to me."

"Nigga I should kill you right now! You come in here joking and speaking on the same woman you kidnapped and had raped like everything cool between us!" I screamed through clenched teeth.

"See that's where your wrong my baby. You've known me all my life and you know I don't condone harming females, let alone raping them. My nation doesn't bleed like that, that's going against everything we stand on. You don't know how angry I was when I found out Autumn was raped! At first I wanted to kill the individual who raped her myself, but I showed major discipline. I sat back and pondered deeply on the situation, and came up with the conclusion that you would probably want his blood as bad as I want it," Slime stood to his feet and begins walking around the office again. He walked pass Ace and Mel, and slid up behind Lo-Lo. In one swift motion Slime pulled out a .50 caliber Dessert Eagle, and pressed it to the back of Lo-Lo's head.

"Now Gino I don't usually discuss what goes on within my nation, but some boundaries have been crossed and laws have been violated. Lo-Lo isn't who you think he is," Lo-Lo stood stiffly with his gun still pointed towards the goons.

I stood there confused with my gun now pointed at Slime. What the fuck he meant Lo-Lo wasn't who he said he was? I been knowing him for 10 years, I know who he is!

"You see…," Slime continued. "Lo-Lo is not only a friend of yours but also a friend of mines too. I met him through a friend that was in prison with him a few years ago, and we became cool. When that shooting at the club took place Lo-Lo had no idea he was shooting at my people until the next day. Once he did find out, he called me and we met up and talked about what had transpired. Since he honestly didn't know, I gave him a pass under one condition which was to inform me on y'all conversations concerning me and my peoples. He was also present when Autumn was kidnapped, and it turns out he was the culprit that raped her while the others were asleep. The only reason I'm telling you this and jeopardizing my inside informant is because he raped Autumn, he violated universal laws, and last but not least…he's infected with HIV-"

"Nigga you outa yo muthafucking mind, don't listen to him Gino! You know me bro; I don't even get down like that! He tryna play mind games with you," Lo-Lo stood up for himself, but it was hard to determine who was telling the truth.

"Oh I'm lying, huh? You disowning the principles you stand on? You disowning your nation?" Slime asked Lo-Lo but got no reply. "I guess I gotta prove my case, huh? Lo-Lo if you so much as move a nerve I'm go blow everything you learned in high school all over this marble table," Slime reached around and stuck his hand in Lo-Lo's front right pocket and pulled out some type of small electronic device.

Slime held the device in the air and I had to strain my eyes to make out what it was, but after a short inspection it was clearly a palm size recorder, and my heart dropped to my stomach.

"To all that still don't know what this is, it's a recorder. I knew this meeting was taking place the moment Gino called Lo-Lo and informed him. I told him to take the recorder and record the whole meeting for me," Slime pushed a button and the recorder came to life,

'…but none of that shit means anything if we don't get our well-deserved respect. As of now the Red Mafiya don't respect us…'

I just stood there in awe; I couldn't believe that Lo-Lo turned out to be the flaw! A nigga I've been knowing, trusting, and loyal to since I met him in Juvenile when we were 14 years old! This bitch was working with the enemy, or in his case, working for his nation! Not only did he betray me, he raped my fucking sister, and was the reason she committed suicide! My heart rate sped up and all kind of thoughts raced through my mind that I literally got dizzy trying to grasp them all at

156

once. This whole time he was acting like he was my boy, and he was the reason Autumn was dead. You couldn't trust anybody in this day and time!

I glanced over at Ace and he had a single tear slowly rolling down his face with a menacing look in his eyes that I've never seen before staring directly at Lo-Lo. I turned my attention back to Slime, and he had the same devilish grin plastered on his face.

"Put it on your flag that everything you said about Lo-Lo is authentic," I dared Slime. One thing I knew for sure is that Slime never lied on his flag, even when we were young I could take his word for it every time he put something on his flag.

"Giovanni Irby Jr., I put it on my flag that Lo-Lo raped your sister and gave her HIV, need I say more? I'm sorry about Autumn's demise, I really am. And the only compensation I could offer you and your family is the man responsible for her death. I know you still probably want to kill me and I can't blame you, but please make the right decision. We already lost one precious life-"with lightning speed Lo-Lo turned around to aim his gun at Slime, but he was shot in the leg before he had the chance to squeeze his trigger. He dropped his gun and grabbed his leg. His leg was leaking blood profusely.

"FUCK-FUCK! AAAGGGHHH! YOU SHOT ME…IN MY FUCKING…LEG!" Lo-Lo screamed curled up on the floor.

"Shut yo duck-ass up you fuck nigga! You gotta move faster than a crack head to take me out!" Slime screamed back.

"Murda, go out there and shut the place down right now! Tell Steve to stick around and clean up," I instructed Murda.

Lo-Lo was still on the floor still whimpering like a bitch. If he thought he was in pain now then he was in for a rude awakening! I scanned the many faces in the room a realized everybody still had their guns pointed at each other ready for a blood bath.

"You can leave Lo-Lo right there, I can handle it from here," I told Slime, walking over to Lo-Lo and picking up the gun he dropped.

"I can respect that, but we'll get rid of this nigga if you want us to," offered Slime.

"I said we got it," I firmly repeated myself.

"Okay I'll leave as I came, in peace. Remember what I said Gino, make the right decision. I'll see you on the other side Lo-Lo. Tell all my enemies I said I still love them," said Slime smiling at the wounded Lo-Lo.

Before leaving he let out a demonic laugh, and his soldiers followed suite as they left the office as one. Not until they were gone and the door was closed behind them did we lower our guns in relief. I leaned over Lo-Lo and smashed him in the head with the butt of my pistol, knocking him completely unconscious. Ace followed suit and began to beat him vehemently just as Murda walked back in the room with a wide-eyed Steve.

"Oh my-maybe I should just leave," Steve stammered, turning to walk out of the office, but Murda stopped him in his tracks, pressing a gun to the back of his head.

"Now Steve, how did those men just barge in this office without permission?" I asked him.

"I don't kn-know, I tri-tried to stop them but-"I slapped the stuttering Steve with an open hand to silence his pitiful plea.

"Mel and Smurf, take this white boy to the basement. Mitch and Murda drag this bitch Lo-Lo down there too," they each followed my instructions and got them both out of my sight leaving Ace and I alone.

I was beyond hurt by Lo-Lo's disloyalty and betrayal, but I could tell Ace was devastated by the distant look in his eyes. They always said it be the ones close to you that will hurt you the most.

"You straight bro?" I asked Ace, and he responded with a head shake. "Come on, we about to make a 'SAW' movie with them fuck niggaz! Grab a pool stick."

Chapter Fourteen

Gino

"**I** See it didn't take you long to forget I existed. I haven't seen you since you came back to pick that money up," said Nadia with a nasty attitude.

I was eating lunch with her at London Chop House on Congress Street downtown. I couldn't get upset at her because she was absolutely right, I've been going through so much lately that I did forget about her and she didn't deserve that type of treatment from any man. Not to mention I just tortured and killed her cousin two days ago, and left his body to rot in the pool hall basement right beside Steve's corps. I doubt if their bodies were discovered yet because Nadia would've been crying a river since he was her favorite cousin.

"I told you I'm sorry, baby girl. But you have to understand I just had to bury my little sister two days ago. I've been going through a lot so don't act like I just neglected you intentionally. You just don't know how bad I missed you girl," I reached across the table and grabbed Nadia's hand.

"I missed you too, baby! I'm sorry about your sister too."

"Don't be, she in a better place. You heard from lo-Lo?"

"Nope, he hasn't called in about a week. You haven't heard from him?"

"Nawl I ain't seen him since my sister funeral. I tried chirping him but he not answering his fucking phone," I responded, taking a bite of my steak tartar dish.

"That's unusual of him, let me try calling him real quick," she said with a concerned look on her face.

Nadia reached into her Chanel handbag to retrieve her Nextel and begin to dial Lo-Lo's number. I sat there and waited on the response I knew she would give me because if Lo-Lo answered his phone it was a trick to it!

"It went straight to voicemail…," she finally replied, and then left a quick message. "Lo-Lo whenever you get this message call me right away, bye."

"Yeah, I've been getting his voicemail too! When he call you back let me know," I waved the waitress over to our table and asked for the bill.

After I paid the bill I escorted Nadia to her car in the parking lot. The day was scorching hot with not a cloud in sight.

"Tomorrow we can spend some time together, so keep your busy schedule free for yo boy, aight?"

"You know I always got free time for you. I'll be looking forward to it though, don't stand me up," Nadia leaned in and gave me a modest kiss on the lips before climbing into her car.

"I can't afford to stand you up, I know that pussy wet right now!"

"Let me see your hand," I stuck my hand through her window and she guided it under her sun dress.

She wasn't wearing any panties so my fingers touched her pulsating moist pussy lips with no interference. I stuck two fingers inside of her and she gasped at my tender touch. I pulled my hand from under her dress and licked my two fingers causing her to become hornier.

"You might want to pull off because I'm tempted to get in that car and fuck your brains loose!" I said, taking a step back from her car.

"Don't threaten me with a good time!" she said as she licked her full tips.

"Get up outta here, I'll be through there tonight! Just keep that muthafucka wet."

I can do that for you. I'll see you tonight, baby," Nadia waved and finally pulled off into traffic.

I walked over to my AUDI A7 and drove off into the packed downtown traffic. My mind drifted back to that hoe nigga Lo-Lo, and thought about how killing him didn't ease my pain, nor feed my hunger to kill

Slime. Earlier, I called my goon James who was the leader of the ruthless Flint Murder team, and informed him that it was a million dollar tag on his head but I wanted him brought to me alive. I gave him all the information I had on Slime, and he relayed the message to his comrades so now it was a waiting process.

I pulled up to a red light on Gratiot and Van Dyke and came to a slow stop. I had the music low and the AC on high because it was close to 95 degrees outside, the highest temperature of the summer so far. I checked all my mirrors and noticed that a navy blue Dodge Caravan was approaching the light on my left side. Once the van stopped right beside me, I looked over at the van and it was occupied by two Mexicans, and the one on the passenger side looked at me and nodded. I returned the nod and focused my attention back on the red light that seemed to take forever to change.

Out of my periphery I could see the side door to the van slide open, but by the time I looked over shots were fired into my door! I instantly ducked down and hit the gas pedal as bullets riddled the side of my car! I didn't know if the light turned green or not but soon found out once my car was struck on the passenger side causing my car to do a full spin! The impact of the crash got glass in my eyes, but the shooting finally stopped and I managed to look up through bloody eyes to see the van speeding off down Van Dyke.

My car was in the middle of the intersection disabled so I opened the driver side door and fell to the scorching hot cement. I tried to stand up but my legs wouldn't cooperate!

"Damn dog, is you straight?" a stranger asked me. My whole body was in pain and blood was everywhere, but all I could think about was the gun under the seat.

"Yeah, I'll be good...," I spit a glob of blood on the cement. "...grab that pistol under my seat and get rid of it for me. I ain't tryna go back to the can my nigga," I replied spitting out more thick blood that tried to choke me.

I could hear police sirens quickly approaching the scene, and I needed this stranger to grab the burner before they got here.

"I got you my nigga, just be still the ambulance is on its way," he said before he leaned in my car and reached under the seat, grabbed the gun and discreetly tucked it on his waist without anyone seeing him.

Once I knew I didn't have to wake up with a weapons case, I lost consciousness and my head slapped the pavement.

*****

I woke up in a cold sweat feeling weak and drowsy to the sound of monitors beeping rhythmically. My eyelids felt as if they weighed five pounds each, and my body felt like it was beat by a mob of football players. I had to remember why I felt this way, and everything came back to me in a flash…somebody tried to kill me! I finally wrestled my eyelids open to see my Mama, Ace, and Zaria hovering over me with concerned looks on their faces. I gave them a weak smile that made me cringe in pain.

"Boy, if it ain't one thing or another. You need to go sit yourself down somewhere and get your priorities together because I'm not trying to bury another child of mine, do you understand Mr. Giovanni?" she asked me sternly.

"Yes Ma'am," I answered with a hoarse voice.

"Good. The doctor said that you're going to be alright, and they plan to release you tomorrow morning. I'll be here in the morning before you leave so get some rest, I love you."

"I love you too," my Mama kissed me on the forehead, and walked out of the room.

Zaria grabbed my hand and I could see she was holding back tears. I squeezed her little hand with as much force as I could muster, and then pulled her closer to me.

"You had me so worried about you, baby! Thank God you're still alive because I don't know what I'll do without you," she whimpered.

"Stop all that crying, girl. Everything good so stop tripping. How long have I been here?" I asked Ace.

"A little over five hours, what the fuck happened?" asked Ace.

I lifted my left arm to scratch my face, and noticed that a bandage was on my arm and shoulder. It was obviously the result s of gunshot wounds, but I didn't even know I was hit! Before I could answer Ace question, a doctor strolled into the room with a clipboard in his hand.

"Hello Mr. Irby, I am Dr. Swordson. I'm glad to see that you're finally awake, and your vitals seem to be good. I took x-rays of all six of your bullet wounds and nothing was too severe or life threatening. You were shot twice in your left leg, once in your left thigh, once in your left calf muscle, once in your left bicep and shoulder, but all the bullets were in and out. There were also grazes on the back of your neck which only left a minor burn on the surface of your skin. There were no major injuries caused by the car accident, just minor cuts from the shattered glass that nicked your eyes and face. Other than that you are perfectly fine, but we will be holding you twenty-four hours for observations. Do you have any questions? How do you feel?

"I feel like shit. Will everything heal properly? I asked the doctor.

"Yes it will heal properly as long as you take care of your wounds."

"Thanks doc, I appreciate your service."

"It's no problem Mr. Irby; I'm just doing my job. On another topic, the police wanted to talk to you earlier but I dismissed that thought being that you were heavily sedated. But they will be returning soon to question you about what took place, so I'll let you know before I allow them in your room," the doctor scribbled something on the paper attached to his clipboard, and then exited the room.

"Zaria, step out in the hallway for a few minutes so I can talk to Ace before the police show up."

"Okay baby, I'll be right outside of the door if you need me. I love you," she leaned in and gave me a quick kiss.

"I love you too, girl," once Zaria was gone and the door was shut behind her, I looked over at Ace and he was standing near the window looking at the sunset.

"So tell me what happened, Gino…everything," he said still facing the window.

"I had lunch downtown with Nadia-"

"Who is Nadia?"

"Remember the chick I met at the mall my first day out?" I reminded him.

"Oh yeah, you talking about Lo-Lo cousin, right?"

"Yeah, I had lunch with her."

"Damn, I ain't even know you were still fucking with her. Does she know Lo-Lo dead?"

167

"Hell nawl, I don't think they found the bodies yet. But any way's, after we had lunch I walked her to her car, and then got in mine once she pulled off. I had been driving up Gratiot for a while because I made it all the way to Van Dyke. When I stopped at the red light on Van Dyke, I peeped a navy blue Caravan approaching my left side. When they stopped at the light next to me I looked over and seen two Mexicans in the van, the one on the passenger side nodded at me. I diverted my attention back to the light but felt something wasn't right, and then outta the corner of my eye I seen the back door slide open. Before I could do anything, they start spraying up the whole driver's side. I ducked down low as I could and stepped on the gas pedal while the light was still red, and got smacked by a truck causing my car to spin all the way around. They continued shooting after I was hit for a few seconds, and then they took off down Van Dyke."

"You ain't have a banger?" asked Ace, still looking out of the window.

"You know I had a pistol, but it was under my seat. When I saw that the van sped off, I got outta the car and fell to the street. Some nigga came over to me trying to help me out, and I told my mans to grab the burner and get rid of it for me. Once I seen him handle that, I fucked around and passed out," I reached over to the table next to me and grabbed the bottle water. After drinking the whole bottle, I continued. "I'll tell you one thing…it wasn't the Red Mafiya."

168

"Why you say that? Who else could it be?" asked Ace, finally turned around to look at me.

"Blood business is Blood business," I vaguely answered.

"What the fuck does that mean?"

"Bloods handle their own affairs, thy never involve outsiders."

"How do you know that the two Mexicans weren't bloods?" asked Ace as if he had a valid question.

"Because I know the Mexican that was driving...," I calmly answered.

"Wha-what...? How do you know him?" asked a surprised Ace, but right before I could answer him, the door was opened by Dr. Swordson stepping into the room.

"You have two detectives' that are here to speak with you, Mr. Irby."

"Thank you for the heads up, you can send them in," I informed the doctor. "Aye bro, get up outta here before those pigs come in. I don't want them to get familiar with you," I told Ace.

"I'll be back in about thirty minutes," said Ace as he made his speedy exit.

A few moments later two black detectives in street clothes entered my room, one looked as if he was in his mid-forties, and the other one in his late twenties. They looked around the room as if I was concealing something within the vicinity, and then each of them took a stance on both sides of the bed.

"Hello Mr. Irby my name is detective Willis, and the man to your left is Detective Camby. We would like to ask you a few questions concerning the shooting that took place earlier today," said the older detective.

"Do I need my lawyer present?" I asked to see their expression, but they gave none.

"Is there a reason to have your lawyer present?" asked the same detective.

'I don't know, that's why I'm asking you."

"I don't see it necessary since your aren't being charged with anything. Do you find it necessary?"

"Not at all, you can proceed."

"Great, so you just got out of prison recently, correct?"

"Correct."

"Could you tell me what happened earlier today, Mr. Irby?"

"Sure. Somebody shot my car up, I drove into traffic and my car was struck," I answered as simply as I could.

"Do you know who shot you?"

"No I don't."

"Why were you shot at?"

"Don't know," I answered quickly as he asked. I could tell Detective Camby didn't like my answers because he let out a dramatic sigh.

"Have you had any altercations with anyone lately," asked Detective Camby.

"No."

"Do you have any beef with anybody, maybe an old enemy before you went to prison?"

"Now that you mention it, I do have beef with a gang," I could tell that my answer sparked an interest in the detective, thinking he had a possible lead.

"Okay, that's a great start. What is the name of this gang?"

"The Police Department," I answered bluntly, and they were fuming!

"I see you think you're a fucking comedian! I don't have time to waste, since you don't want to help capture the muthafucka's that tried to kill you, I hope they succeed next time! But let me ask you this, how could you afford to drive a brand new AUDI A7 and you were just released from prison months ago," asked Detective Willis.

"My retained lawyer name is Sam Cooper; his number is 586-555-2125. Maybe you could call him and ask him how I can afford a car that cost more than your yearly salary," that remark hit them hard, but what could they do to me?

"If you decide to help yourself, here's my card. But we will be watching you very closely you arrogant son-of-a-bitch," said Detective Camby, sitting his card at the foot of my bed.

"I'm glad to hear that, now I feel safe, but I must warn you, don't watch me too closely because those harassment lawsuits are strenuous," I replied smiling at the two agitated officers.

Without even responding they stormed out of the room upset that they wasted their precious time. I sat up and grabbed the card with my right hand and ripped it to little pieces. Wasn't an ounce of rat in my blood!

***

Woke up the next morning in even more pain; I guess the heavy dose of morphine wore off. The gunshot wounds were throbbing, but I still couldn't wait to leave this depressing hospital. Just laying here all day drained my energy, and had me feeling down. I know I'm not supposed to be happy but damn!

After the dick sucking detectives left yesterday, Ace returned and I told him about how I knew one of the Mexicans, and he couldn't believe it. I explained to him how when the van pulled up and I looked at the driver I thought he looked vaguely familiar, but I couldn't figure out where I knew him from. I didn't realize who the Mexican was until I was already shot and laying in the middle of the street.

The Mexican that was driving name was, Lucky. He was very close friends and business partner of our dearly departed, Mook! I knew the lick I killed Mook for was too good and easy to be true. I learned at a young age that to every action comes a reaction, but not only was I on a mission to kill Slime; I had to worry about the ruthless Mexican Mafia! Somehow and some way, I had to overcome this obstacle fast or I'll be dead any day now. When it rains, it pours.

I was lost deep in my thought when I heard a knock at my door, and it slowly opened before I could say come in. I was surprised to see who walked through the door.

"Hey baby, how are you doing?" asked Destiny as she sashayed over to me with balloons in her hand and a card, and kissed me on the cheek.

She was wearing a white conservative Versace jumpsuit, with matching stiletto's. No matter how much pain I was in, my dick still became aroused at her sexy chic attire.

"Damn girl, I'm doing even better now that you've blessed me with your presence! I can't believe you're here, how you find out?"

"You were on the news-well you weren't on the news but your car was. I called your phone and you didn't answer, I called every surrounding hospital until I found you. I figured your family and girlfriend would be

173

here yesterday, so I decided to pop up today. I was so scared…,"
Destiny became real emotional and tears started streaming down her
face.

"Come here, baby," I hugged Destiny, and her whole body was shaking
as she continued to cry her heart out. "Sssh, stop all that crying…I'm
straight Destiny, I ain't going anywhere."

"Just promise me Gino… promise me you'll never leave me," she
demanded, looking dead in my eyes.

"I promise you," there I was making another promise that I couldn't
possibly keep. I couldn't predict the future, or avoid the grim reaper, so
how could I promise such a thing? As long as God knew my heart was
in the right place, I felt no guilt.

I released Destiny and grabbed the card out of her hand. I opened the
card and read it to myself,

'Love never dies of starvation, but often of indigestion.'

I sat there and thought deeply, trying to wrap my mind around the quote.
It didn't take but a minute to fully comprehend the meaning behind the
message, and I couldn't even explain the emotion I felt from within my
heart, but I knew I fell deeper in love with Destiny. I knew I had a lot of
love for her, but I just realized that I was also in love with her.

I was shocked out of my trance by the sound of the door opening, and Zaria walking in the room with a smile that quickly vanished once she spotted Destiny standing by my bedside.

"What's up baby, you remember Destiny don't you?" I asked in an attempt to make light of the situation.

"Why is she here?" she asked me but starred at Destiny.

"I was just-," Destiny tried to explain but was quickly cut off."

"I wasn't talking to you bitch, so shut the fuck up!" yelled Zaria.

"Who the fuck you think you calling a bitch, BITCH!" Destiny yelled back as she released the balloons and got into a fighting stance. I quickly intervened before it got out of hand.

"Both of y'all need to chill the fuck out right now!" I had to raise my voice to get their attention. "Destiny can you please leave so I can talk to my girl. I'll call you when I get a chance," I politely told her.

"I can respect that, and I apologize if I caused any confusion. I hope you get well soon, be sure to call me," she replied while starring at Zaria.

After the brief stare down, she finally walked past Zaria and out of the door. I knew I was in for a tongue lashing so I prepared myself mentally.

"I can't believe you have the fucking nerves to have one of your hoes up in here knowing I could pop up at any minute," Zaria had her arms folded across her chest clearly upset and on the brink of tears.

"I don't know why you come in here causing a scene when I already told you that she was Autumn's friend-"

"She was Autumn's friend my ass, Gino! Stop fucking lying to me like I'm stupid!" her tears were flowing now.

"You need to stop fucking yelling and calm the fuck down!"

"You know what... fuck you, Gino! I can't stand yo dog-ass!" she continued to yell, I was too sore and too tired to argue back, I was done.

"Go home, Zaria," I said calmly.

"I'm not going anywhere until I get an explanation," she replied defiantly

"I said get the fuck out and go home BITCH! GO HOME!" I had lost all patience with her; I never call her out of her name. She stood there with her mouth wide open in shock that I called her a bitch for the first time. She stood frozen for a few seconds, and then ran out of the room crying hysterically! As she ran out of the room and brushed past my Mama who so happen to be coming in. "What the hell is the matter with that girl?" she asked me with confusion.

"She'll be alright, can you please get me outta here so I can get some real rest,"

Chapter Fifteen

Gino

It's been two days since I was discharged from the hospital, and I was definitely feeling better physically, but distraught mentally. Zaria was still mad at me about the Destiny Incident, so she wasn't talking to me unless she absolutely had to. I didn't mind the silent treatment; I needed the quite time to evaluate how my life became so hectic in such a short time period.

The main thing I wanted to know was how did the Mexican Mafia know that I robbed and killed Mook? I'm pretty sure I didn't leave any evidence, or clues? I wonder if he had hidden cameras in the house. Highly unlikely because the police wasn't looking for me. Did Mook call Lucky before I got there to inform him I was on my way to meet him? Could be the case, but if it wasn't somebody that's close to me had to tip them off and I was on a mission to find out who.

I had a close Mexican confidant that lived on the southwest side of Detroit, and he knew almost everything that transpired in this community. Poncho was a high ranking member of the Latin Counts, and controlled majority of the illegal activity on the southwest side which was known for its violent Latin street organizations. I decided to give him a call to see what he knew about my current situation. The phone rang a few times before he finally answered.

"Speak," he answered with a heavy Spanish accent.

"What's up Poncho, this Gino?"

"Hey Gino! I haven't heard from you in a long time, how are you doing my friend? I'm glad to see you're still alive."

"I'm doing much better big homie, but I'll be doing a lot better if you could guide me in the right direction," I said getting straight to the point.

"I'm really hurt that you only call when you need something from me, Gino. You are para Sempre a friend of me so quien nos separa us? What do you need to know?' asked Poncho.

"Come on Poncho, don't say it like that! You know you are forever a friend of mine too, and no one can separate us," I replied, letting him know my Spanish wasn't rusty.

"I'm glad to hear that, now we can talk."

"I'm sure you already know what's going on with me."

"Absolutely! Being an enemy of Lucky isn't a good look. And from my understanding he was present when they tried to kill you which mean that he personally wants to kill you. And then being an enemy of Slime is a whole different battlefield."

"Yeah I know that much. So what I need to know is how did Lucky find out who killed and robbed Mook?" I could hear Poncho take a deep breath on the other end of the phone.

"Gino, Gino, Gino…. You got a lot to learn about the type of business you're invested in. Nobody is to be trusted…NOBODY! I'm going to do you a solid favor, you hear me? He asked me.

"Yeah, I hear you Poncho."

"I'm going to let you figure this one out on your own."

"Huh…? What you mean?" I asked, not quite sure I heard him correct.

"I need you to trust me on this one my friend. I got a lot of faith in you, so I know you will figure it out before its' too late. The only thing I will tell you is vivora en el sacate desde la cuana. Think about it hard and then don't just react, respond quietly. Amor"

"Amor, Poncho," and then our phone conversation came to an end.

I sat there and tried my hardest to analyze what he, just told me, and that helped me narrow it down to only a few people. Something real grimy was going on, but the truth will come to the light eventually.

I climbed out of the bed and put most of my weight on the right side of my body. The shot to the calf did the most damage to my leg, and made me walk with a slight limp. I walked slowly to the living room where Zaria was laying on the couch watching a Tyler Perry play called *'Diary of a mad black woman'*. I looked at her facial expression and couldn't help but to laugh. She looked up at me irritated and confused.

"Something funny?" she asked me but I continued to laugh causing her to suck her teeth and roll her eyes.

I finally got control of myself, limped over to the flat screen plasma TV and unplugged every single plug in the outlet.

"Why you watching that stupid ass play?"

"Because I like the fucking play, do I come in here unplugging shit when you watching stupid ass sports?"

"So you're watching the play because you like it, or because you can relate to it?"

"What does it matter, Gino?" Just let me watch what I want to watch and leave me the fuck alone!"

"You can't watch that bullshit because you're not a mad black woman no matter how hard you try to portray it!"

"What…? You know what, fuck you okay…?" Zaria got up from the couch and tried to plug the TV back in but I stood in front of the socket.

"Gino, moooove!" she whined trying to push me out of the way with all her might, but I wouldn't budge.

The more aggressive and frustrated she became the more attractive she became to me! I finally grabbed her by her arms and pulled her body close to mine, and stuck my tongue down her throat. She was reluctant at first, but once I got a firm grip on her ass, she became submissive. We continued the groping and kissing session for almost five minutes straight before I broke our kiss, and looked her in the eyes.

"You love me Zaria?" I asked seriously.

"You know I love you."

"Would you do anything to hurt me?" I asked. She hesitated for a second before she answered.

"Baby, of course I wouldn't. Why you ask me that?" When she asked me that I knew she was hiding something from me. Any typical person will get offended when you ask them an uncharacteristic question, not ask you why. I knew Zaria loved me, but I didn't know what she loved more than me.

"Don't worry about it baby, I just asked. Now let's get to the room so I can knock them walls down!" She grabbed my hand and led me to the bedroom, and all I could ask myself was, am I sleeping with the enemy?"

The next morning I received the dreadful call I was waiting on from Nadia. She called me at noon crying a river, letting me know that they found Lo-Lo dead in the basement of his pool hall. In all, it took them 72 hours to find his body, and I knew it was probably deteriorated badly! I played my role and made it seem like I was surprised and hurt about the discovery, but the Lord knew I could give two fucks!

She then begins to tell me how he was raped with a pool stick, and they found half the pool stick still stuck in his ass! She also enlightened me that he was shot over thirty-two times in the face, disfiguring and crushing every bone, so they had to have a closed casket.

Nadia wanted me to come over to console her, but I had to explain that I was shot up the other day and I had to stay on bed rest. She didn't know anything about the incident so she started crying all over again. After asking me a series of questions, I convinced her that I was alright; I told her that I was sending somebody over to bring her enough money to cover all funeral costs. She cried for a few more minutes, and then I had to end our conversation. If this chick wasn't the most emotional woman in the world it was a trick to it.

I got right back on the phone and called my ride or die chick, Destiny.

"Hey baby! I miss you so much!" She squealed once she answered the phone.

"I miss you too, sexy. What you been up to?"

"Nothing much but waiting on you to call. I just got out of the shower, and was getting ready to go to my real estate class. How have you been?"

"I been well, letting my body heal. I'm glad to hear you started your classes, ain't nothing more sexy than a woman with goals and a bright future. And you gotta be the sexiest woman alive!"

"Boy shut up!" Destiny replied while laughing, her laugh was soothing to my soul.

I had a feeling that me and Destiny had a thing that would last a lifetime. Everything about her was one hundred percent authentic. Her personality, her aura, and most importantly her feelings for me had me thinking about making her my main bitch, but leaving Zaria was out of the question as of now.

"I need you to do something for me."

"Name it," she replied eagerly.

"I need you to get twenty thousand out of the safe, and drop it off to this address so go grab a pen," I gave her Nadia's address with instructions to deliver it before sunset.

"She will be expecting you baby, so be on time. Can you handle that?"

"Of course I can, I got you boo! When are you coming to see me?" she asked causing my dick to jerk!

Believe it or not, Destiny and I still haven't had sex yet. We almost did on a few occasions but she always told me she wasn't ready.

I respected her decision, therefore I never pushed her I let her set the pace. But I knew one thing; I was so ready to experience what it would be like that whenever she did give me the cookies, she will remember me forever.

"Give me a couple days to get my priorities together, and then we can spend as much time together as you want. Okay?"

"You promise?"

"I promise."

"Gino?"

"Yeah baby."

"I love you," she whispered, and I smiled even harder than a musician winning a Grammy.

"I love you too."

I had Zaria go pick me up a rental car from Enterprise so I could take care of business, and not to mention I was tired of being stuck in the fucking condo all day. I was healing as expected, but my left leg was still kind of weak and tender. I would fight through the pain because I had shit to take care of immediately.

I told her to bring me back something fast but low-key, so she brought me back a 2004 Chevy Trial blazer SS. As soon as she came back I informed her that my homie Lo-Lo was dead, and I was on my way to his family house. She bought my story and I was out of the door in a flash.

Once I got in the truck I called my exterminator James and told him to gather the murder team and meet me at the safe house the house I had ducked off on the Westside. He agreed and told me he'll be there ASAP, so I hung up the phone with him and called Ace.

"What's up big bro, what's the word?" asked Ace after answering his phone.

"Ain't shit up, just laying low? How the business doing?"

"You know business is business, everything booming. I got about five days of your earnings bagged up; you want me to bring it to yo condo?"

"Nawl, I'll have Murda come pick it up and take it to the Boston District," I told him.

"You over there? Or are you on your way over there? Because if you are I can drop it off myself," Ace volunteered.

"Nawl, I'm posted at the crib," I lied.

"Alright, let me know when yo man's coming through."

"Alright, I'll pop at you later."

"Aye, when we go sit down and talk about how we gone handle the current events?" asked Ace.

"Gimme a couple days to rest up, then we'll get the team together."

"I'm holding shit down until then, make sure you get at me," and our conversation ended.

I finally pulled into the six bedroom, four baths, three story safe house driveway on W. Boston and LaSalle Street. I drove all the way into the backyard and parked the truck in front of the two car garage. James and his team hadn't arrived yet, so I took that extra time to make sure everything was still intact. I checked the money I had stashed in the dining room under the floor board, and everything was counted for. I was so paranoid after almost being killed, I looked out of the window every sixty seconds to see if everything was safe as I cradled my Smith & Wesson .11 millimeter.

After a fifteen minute wait, James finally arrived three cars deep. I counted each one of them as they got out and it was a total of seven of them. I opened the front door and greeted all of them with a pound as they entered.

"My nigga James, what up with you playboy?" I said giving him a firm handshake.

"You know me Gino; I'm focused on completing that mission for you. I'm glad to see that you survived that hit. Was that Slime call?" asked James as I led the way to the basement.

"Yeah that was that fuck nigga," I lied.

"So you know we about to put in overtime."

"Ain't no doubt, added one of his comrades?

Once we all was in the basement I flicked the switch on the furnace up, and it took a few seconds to come alive making a loud buzzing noise. I turned the furnace on to drown out our conversation just in case the house was bugged. I learned this tactic from watching an episode of the Sopranos. I cleared my throat, and started the meeting.

"Listen, I know y'all niggas good at what you do, and y'all been hard at work. But I need y'all to pick up the momentum and deliver Slime to me, matter of fact, just on sight that nigga. Whenever you spot him, drop him, and come collect y'all money. I don't even care about killing him myself anymore, just get the job done. I'm raising the ticket to one and a half million, dead or alive. I just want this to happen within a week, can y'all handle that?"

"Shiiittt, for one and a half milli we ain't got no choice. That means we all get two-hundred grand a piece at the least. Duke said astounded who was James lil brother.

"Yeah my nigga…," James spoke up. "…we got you bro. That nigga slime outta there on sight," his whole team agreed and became rowdy at the thought of having all that money.

"I'm glad y'all motivated, let's get the job done."

Chapter Sixteen

Ace

H ow you don't know where the fuck your man at?" I asked Zaria.

"Because he a grown-ass man and he can go anywhere he pleases. Why are you so concerned about it anyway?" snapped Zaria.

"I was just –I'm just worried about him. You know somebody already tried to kill him, how can I protect him if I don't know where he at?" I replied calmly.

We were chilling at my house in the living room watching the movie Scarface. I had a plate full of powder cocaine on the table that I periodically sniffed a line from. I picked up the habit a few weeks ago, and was able to hide it from everybody except Mitch, and now Zaria.

"You need to stop snorting that stuff because it's making you crazy," Zaria told me, looking at me in disgust.

"Don't knock anything unless you try it yourself. Besides, you don't be complaining when I put this dope dick in you, do you?" She smiled and shook her head no.

I picked up my rolled up hundred dollar bill, and leaned over the table. I made two thick white lines with the razor blade, and snorted one line in each nostril. I sat the bill down, stood up in front of Zaria while unbuckling my pants, and pulled out my already hard dick. I stroked it a few times in front of her and could see the desire burning in her eyes.

"You want me in your mouth, don't you? Here, put it in your mouth," She leaned forward and grabbed the shaft of my throbbing erection, and kissed just the tip of it. She knew that drove me crazy.

After teasing for a minute, she inserted into her warm mouth and slowly sucked my dick like it was the last dick on earth. I knew her pussy was getting wet by the second because her legs begin to shake involuntary. In mid stroke, I took a step back leaving Zaria looking lost. I sat back down next to her, picked up the razor blade, and begin to make more lines.

"What are you doing?" she asked becoming frustrated. "Can you hurry up so we can fuck?"

"Yeah, we can fuck as soon as you…," I paused for a few seconds to pick up the hundred dollar bill, and then I held it out for her to grab it. "…snort a few lines," I said in more of a demand that a question.

"Ace, I'm not about to snort nothing, so stop playing with me and come here," she reached over to grab my dick, but I slapped her hand away from it.

"Oww boy that hurt. Stop playing with me Ace."

"I'm not playing with you, so here…," I tried to hand her the bill again.

"No ace. You are not about to have me addicted to cocaine like I'm a fucking fiend or something."

'You're not going to be addicted. Just try it one time, and I promise you won't be addicted."

"How do you know that?"

"Didn't I encourage you to smoke weed? Did you like it?"

"Yeah but that's only weed."

"Are you addicted to weed?"

"No," she answered hesitantly.

"Okay then. This shit ain't no different, trust me. And it's going to make you feel ten times better. Look at my dick, that muthafucka still hard as a Jolly Rancher. So stop playing and hit these lines so I can fuck you like a porno star."

Zaria leaned down, took a deep breath, snorted a line up her left nostril, and then jumped back damn near scaring me.

"Oh my God, it burns Ace. What the fuck?" yelled Zaria grabbing her nose as if that would stop the burning?

I fell over laughing, dick swinging and everything. I was laughing so hard my stomach started to hurt, and I was out of breath. I looked back over at Zaria and she was steaming mad because I was laughing instead of trying to comfort her. Tears were running down my face too, and Zaria punched me in the arm.

"Ace, this shit ain't funny." She whined, and I had to slowly get control of myself.

"Baby it's going to burn when you do it for the first time. Once you do it once in each nostril, it'll never burn again. Do the other line in your other nostril," I instructed her.

Zaria leaned over the table, and snorted the other line but didn't jump or complain this time. I could tell she was buzzing by looking at her glazed eyes. Damn, that coke made her look even sexier. I started stroking my dick, and grabbed Zaria by her neck, guiding her head down to my lap. She was beyond high, but could still function enough to pleasure me. And that's exactly what she did.

***

"Where the fuck is he?"

"I don't fucking know. He hasn't been calling me or anything," I responded honestly, perspiration building on my forehead.

"Ace..," the man spoke in broken English, so you could hardly understand him. "I feel like you coming between me and my money. And when me get that feeling…," he lit up his cigar, and blew out a thick cloud of smoke. "… I kill em. Now, you have to ask yourself whose life is worth more, his or yours?"

I stood in the middle of an abandoned warehouse with the most notorious organization in America, and I was never more terrified in my life but I had to remain calm and in control.

"Listen, I told you the nigga been ducking and dodging me. It's like the nigga vanished or something, what can I do?"

"Tell me where he lives."

"I don't know where the nigga stay, he fucking moved out of Detroit."

"And you don't know where to?"

"No!" I screamed to let them know I was telling the truth.

"If I find out you lie to me… just call me next time you see him.

I don't care where it's at, or what time it is, call me."

Chapter Seventeen

Gino

Exactly two weeks later I got the news I've been waiting patiently to receive. I was at home taking a long shower when I got the call from James.

"Are you sure?" I asked in bewilderment. I was standing in the middle of the bathroom completely naked, dripping water on the tile floor.

"Gino, he outta there my nigga, I would give you the details but I don't talk on the phone cause it might stick," said James with much confidence.

"I can respect that, so you and the team come to the same spot as last time right now," I told James, then ended the call.

I dried my body completely off, and wrapped the towel around my waist. I walked outta the bathroom into the bedroom to find Zaria still fast asleep in the bed. As of lately, she hasn't been acting like herself, and I didn't know what to make of it. She's been real fidgety, and nervous around me, and whenever I pointed it out she blamed it on being tired. Yesterday she wasn't scheduled to work, but she still came in the house at three in the morning with her nursing uniform on as if she just came from work. I called up to her job and asked her supervisor was she at work, and just as I expected she didn't go to work. I didn't even confront her about the situation; I just logged it in my memory.

I hurriedly got dressed, kissed Zaria on the cheek, grabbed my pistol, and practically ran to the parking garage. I got in the rented truck, and drove off into the early morning busy traffic hoping that the news of slime being dead was a dream come true.

I decided to stop at I-Hop to grab me a quick bite to eat because I was hungry as fuck. The cashier that took my order was a short, well proportion, petite, white chick that was about 18 years old. I could look at her and tell that she was attracted to me, but was too shy to say anything. She didn't look me in the eyes for more than two seconds, and then would look at the cash register. I thought it was funny and cute how shy she was, so I decided to play around with her.

"What's your name cutie?"

"Who me?" she asked looking over her shoulder.

"You're the only cute one I see in here," she blushed hard, feeling stupid about her reply. "So what's your name? I asked again.

"Becky," she answered shyly.

"Becky huh? I think you're a sexy woman Becky, how old are you?"

"I'm 18, why you ask me that?" she asked.

"Never mind that, you might be a little too young for me. I apologize for even wasting your time sweetheart," I said to make it seem like I wasn't interested.

"How old are you?" She asked in desperation.

"I'm almost ten years older than you, you can't do anything for a grown man," I lied about my age to see how far she was willing to go to win me over.

"What does that supposed to mean?" she asked with a slight attitude.

"That means I need a grown woman, no offense to you snowflake. I don't think you can handle a man like me."

"How do you know that when you haven't even gave me the opportunity," she gave me a flirtatious smirk.

An older white employee placed my order on the counter, gave me a tight smile, and walked away. Becky slid the tray toward me, and brushed my hand in the process.

"You ever fucked a black guy before?" I asked bluntly.

"No I haven't, but it's a first time for everything."

"Call 555-8216, don't forget it. My name Gino by the way," I leaned over the counter, kissed her on the cheek, grabbed my food, and left her standing there mesmerized.

*****

When I got to the safe house on W. Boston, James was already there with his murder team. I parked in the backyard as usual, and disposed the empty food tray once I got outta the truck. I limped to the front where they were waiting on the porch, and then led everybody into the house and straight to the basement. After turning the furnace switch on, I finally surveyed who all showed up and noticed that somebody was missing.

"Where Duke at?" I asked James.

"I don't know where that lil nigga at. I ain't seen him since we left the bar last night after we did what we did. I tried calling his phone but it went straight to voicemail, must be lying up with a bitch passed out," James explained to me.

"Alright, so tell me what happened," I was eager to hear the story.

"Me, Duke, and Rell was driving up I-94 north bond on our way to Applebee's when I spotted a red Corvette driving on the side of us. I didn't know fosho if it was him or not until I read the license plate. So after seeing the plates, I slowed so he could get in front of us, and then I switched lanes so I was three cars behind him. Just as I expected, the nigga got off at the E. Outer Drive and Harper Ave exit. Duke had a hunnit round drum on a choppa, and me and Rell only had the fifty round clip on our shit. Once he drove past Harper Ave light going down

E. Outer Drive, I sped pass the vette and forced him to crash into a parked car. I blocked the nigga off; we all got outta the car, and sprayed his shit up. After I emptied my clip, I eased up to the car, opened the drivers' door, and Duke started spraying at him again at close range. Ain't' no fucking way dog lived through that shit bro, that's on my ole lady." I just stood there for a moment in amazement; this shit was too good to be true. I couldn't see Slime slipping like that with no type of reinforcement.

"So he ain't have nobody with him, wasn't nobody following him?" I asked in astonishment.

"Hell nawl, he was slipping hard fam." Said Rell.

"Are you sure?" I asked again not quite convinced.

"Yeah "G"! Why you think it ain't possible?" asked James.

"The shit was just too easy for comfort. I guess y'all niggaz make killing a powerful General look easy. I got y'all boys cash upstairs, I'll be right back," I rushed upstairs to the living room and grabbed the two duffel bags off the couch.

I took the two bags to the dining room and lifted the floorboard up where I had my money stashed. Majority of my drug money was stashed here so I didn't have to run around the city to collect money every day. I gave Murda full control of all the spots in Ypsilanti since Lo-Lo was dead, and we made arrangements for him to bring all my money here. I had Smurf collect my money in the city since I got shot up, and he delivered it here too.

The money was in one hundred thousand stacks so I didn't have to keep counting it over and over again. Plus it came in handy when I was purchasing something, I didn't waste any time cashing out. I put fifteen one hundred thousand dollar bands inside the spacious duffel bags, replaced the floorboards, and dragged the two bags down the stairs.

"Here go all the money, even Duke's slice of the pie. I appreciate y'all niggaz service, hit me up if you need anything, and I'll do the same. Be careful with this money, people don't ride around with a million five every day." Everybody laughed at my comment. Not that it was funny, but because they had more money than they ever seen in their life.

I watched everybody pile into their cars, and drive off. Once they were out of sight, I went back in the house praying that they killed the right muthafucka. I wasn't convinced that Slime was dead just yet; I had to do my own research.

I went into the living room and grabbed five duffel bags, and dragged them to the dining room. I lifted the floorboard and begin to stuff each bag until the stash spot was completely empty. Altogether it was 5.3 million dollars in all the bags collectively. I was on my way to Destiny house to have her hold the money for me. She already had five hundred thousand I told her to hold a few days before I got shot up. I figured if she ain't run off with that, she was trustworthy enough to hold this money for me. If she ran off with it, then oh well. But I didn't think she was cut like that, but only time will tell.

I put the bags in the back of the truck one at a time because they were heavy as fuck. After securing the house I got in the car and made my way to Destiny's house.

"About time you came to see me baby, I missed you so much." said Destiny, as she hugged and kissed me passionately.

"I missed you too girl, you just don't know," I responded meaning every word. Destiny looked down and nodded at the one duffel bag I sat on the carpet.

"What's in there?" she asked.

"I'll tell you when I bring the other four bags in. I'll be right back," I kissed her one more time, and went back to the garage to retrieve the other bags.

After I finally got the other bags in the house and up the stairs to the master bedroom, I stretched out across the bed exhausted from the hard labor. Whoever knew carrying money could be a full body workout. Destiny entered the room with a bottle of water, and I instantly drink the whole bottle before she had a chance to sit down.

"You sure were thirsty, you want me to get you another bottle?" she offered.

"Nawl, I'm straight."

"So what's in the bags? I'm assuming it's something heavy by the way you're sweating," Destiny giggled.

"You never lied, I'm tired as fuck." I wiped the sweat on my forehead with the collar of my shirt, and then sat up. "What's in the bags is our future, 5.3 million dollars-"before I could finish my sentence, she cut me off.

"5.3 million dollars? Boy, quit playing." She said in awe.

"I'm serious baby girl."

"Like T.I.?" asked a wide-open Destiny and I couldn't help but to laugh at the same analogy I used on her.

"Yeah, like T.I., baby. You can take a look if you want to," I offered, and she kneeled down on the floor to unzip one of the bags and gasped. She covered her mouth with both of her hands, and looked up at me in shock.

"Who money is this?" she asked perplexed.

"It's our money, and we got plenty more where that came from."

"What do you mean 'ours'?"

202

"I mean exactly what I said, that's our money." I grabbed both of Destiny hands and pulled her towards me. "Listen, I got a lot going on in my life right now, and I don't know how shit might turn out. I want to make sure that you are stable financially."

"Baby, this money won't mean nothing if I don't have you in my life. I don't love money Gino, I love you."

"I know baby that's exactly why I want to be with you," I confessed.

"How is that possible when you're still with Zaria?"

"I'm leaving Zaria."

"Gino, don't just tell me that to make me think its hope between us being a couple. I told you when I first met you that I was willing to deal with you having a girlfriend. So if you're saying this-"

"I don't play games, Destiny. I want to spend the rest of my life with you and I mean that shit. I know I'm not an angel, but for you I'll try to be the best man I can be. I was with Zaria for 15 years, Destiny. It took me 15 years to realize that she's not the one for me. Through adversity she's not as strong as I thought she was, she can't handle pressure," tears started to pour down Destiny's face as I opened up to her. I let go of one of her hands, and wiped away her tears with my thumb. "But you…everything I want in a woman you possess and I pray to God that you never lost it. Just give me a week at the most, then, we can move outta Michigan and begin a new life anywhere you want. Is that cool with you? She couldn't even speak, she just shook her head yes.

"I love you, girl."

"I love you too, baby."

"Can I make love to you tonight?" she shook her head yes again.

"Then take them damn clothes off," I pulled her on top of me as I laid back and kissed her with all the lust I could muster.

Chapter Eighteen

Gino

L̲ater on that day after leaving Destiny's house, I went back home to take a shower and a quick nap. Sex was so intensifying with Destiny that I contemplated if I should go home or not. I knew the experience would be memorable, but I never imagined it would be that magnificent. She was officially the total package for a real nigga, and now she belonged to me.

I was sitting in the living room watching Sports center waiting on Zaria to come home and cook. In the process of waiting, my phone begins to ring, and after looking at the screen I seen it was my Mama.

"What's the word old lady?" I teased her.

"You gone get enough of calling me old, I'm still in my prime and I'm not a grandmother yet. What… you can't get it up you young punk?" My mama snapped on me and I was dying laughing.

"My bad moms, you know I love me some you."

"Yeah, yeah I love you too. When was the last time you talked to Ace?"

"It's been a couple of days, why?"

"Because he called me today saying you won't answer his calls. He thinks you're mad at him about something, so what's going on?"

"Ain't nothing going on Mama, I just forgot to call him back. It ain't intentional, I just been getting rest so I can heal," I lied to my Mama.

The truth was ever since I had that talk with Poncho, I became even more paranoid. I didn't know who gave my name to Lucky so everybody was a suspect in my eyes. But I was thinking to myself earlier, if Ace was the traitor, then why haven't the Mexican Mafia knocked down my front door yet? Ace knew where I rested my head, so it was unlikely that he told them. Not to mention, Ace was my flesh and blood, my only brother at that. Maybe I was tripping, but I was just playing it safe until I figured out who the snake was.

"Oh, okay. You be sure to call that boy, you know he look up to you," she instructed me

"I'm gone call him as soon as I hang up with you."

"You do that, oh yeah, your old friend from the neighborhood stopped by here this morning. He bought me some roses and chocolate too."

"What old friend from the neighborhood?" I asked wondering who and how somebody knew where my Mama lived. It has to be somebody she knew or she would've never opened the door.

"You know the one that stayed down the street in that black and white house… what's his name umm… Marcel." She finally shouted.

"What…?" was all I could say.

"Yeah, he came by here and we talked for about twenty minutes. He's still such a sweetheart, but then again he always was a good kid," my Mama said with admiration.

"Mama, are you sure it was Marcel?" I asked now beginning to panic.

"I'm sure it was him, I know Marcel when I see him, boy. You used to be with that boy every day; you think I don't know who that boy is?"

"Mama, I'm gone call you back later, I got something to take care of right quick."

"Is something wrong?"

"Nawl, everything cool, just don't let Marcel back in your house; don't even open the door for him."

"Why, y'all not friends anymore?"

"You can say that. But I gotta go, talk to you later."

"Okay baby, you be careful," I hung up the phone, and stood up as I dialed James number but got no answer.

What the fuck. I hope my Mama was mistaken and Marcel didn't really show up at her house. Marcel was Slime's real name, and if he popped up at my Mama house then he was sending a message to let me know that it was easy to kill the people close to me. If that was Slime he knew I tried to have him murked and I didn't know the aftermath of it.

Why the fuck was James not answering his phone?" I limped quickly to the bedroom, and grabbed the AR-15 I had stashed under my bed. I made sure it was fully loaded before I started pacing the bedroom floor, but the ringing of my phone halted the pacing. It was James returning my calls.

"Why the fuck you ain't been answering your phone nigga?" I yelled into the receiver.

"I left my phone in the car! Gino, I'm about to start offing everything moving, I swear to fucking God!" James yelled on the other end of the phone.

"James, I don't know what you bitching about Slime ain't dead! He popped up at my OG house today."

"I already know he ain't' dead, them bitches got Duke. They just called talking about they go kill all of us one at a time. I think they already killed Duke Dawg." James was beyond hysterical, and I felt his pain but I had my own problems.

"When did they call?"

"About an hour ago, we just checked into a new hotel, I gotta go look for Duke man, they got my lil brother."

"Calm the fuck down. You can't go in them streets, riding around looking for him because you not gone find him. You gotta wait it out and see what's gone happen. Most likely they gone call you back, if they don't then…," he knew the latter. "If Slime wasn't driving the vette, I wonder who was." I thought out loud.

"I don't know man, but bodies gone continue to drop if I don't get my bro back, and that's my word." And he hung up in my face.

Did James just threaten me? Fuck that nigga, I had other shit to worry about but I wonder how the Red Mafia got Duke in the first place? Man, this shit getting crazier and crazier. I should just take Destiny and take off outta state, but I can't. I had shit I needed to find out before I leave. After I learned what I needed to know, then I'm gone forever. But I had a feeling shit was about to get real bloody.

I woke up the next morning clutching the assault rifle tired as fuck. I probably got two hours of sleep at the most and here it was nine in the morning and somebody ringing my damn doorbell. I swiftly jumped to my feet and slid on my air Jordan's while still holding on the AR-15. Did Slime or the Mexican mafia finally decide to finish the job?"

"I got it, you stay back here," I told Zaria before she made it outta the room.

When I got to the front door I looked through the peephole, and studied the white man in the brown uniform on the other side of the door.

"Fucking UPS man," I mumbled to myself. Zaria probably ordered some more bullshit off the internet, or could this be a setup for me to put my guard down?'

"What up?" I yelled through the door.

"UPS, I have a package for a Mr. Irby." announced the delivery man. Maybe Zaria did order something using my debit card, but I still wasn't taking any chances.

"Leave the package right there and walk away, I'll get it."

"I can't do that sir, it's against company policy, not to mention I need your signature," the white man replied in a matter of fact one.

Damn I leaned the AR-15 against the wall next to the door, and eased the door open with my foot prompted behind it just in case he decided to rush me. I looked up the hallways both ways and it was clearly empty. The UPS man looked at me as if I was insane but if he only knew what I was going through.

"I just need your signature sir, and I'll be on my way," he held out the clip board and I snatched it from him but still watched him closely. I signed it, gave it back to him, and watched him walk away and get on the elevator. When I seen that he was actually gone, I picked up the big and heavy box, and carried it to the living room. After making sure the door was secure, I grabbed the assault rifle, and went back to the bedroom.

Zaria was making up the bed with nothing but a t-shirt on, and to me it looked like she was losing weight. I didn't mention it though because I knew how sensitive women were about their weight. She came in late last night again on her off day. I didn't know if she's been seeing another nigga or not, and I really didn't care. Soon I wouldn't have to worry about her. I would be starting a new life with my future wife Destiny.

"Why are you carrying that big gun around the house?" she asked me looking kind of worried, but I didn't even entertain her question.

"What the fuck you ordered that's so damn heavy? I asked her.

"What I ordered? What are you talking about?"

"The UPS man just dropped a package off."

"I don't think… no I didn't order anything, maybe it's a gift, I'm about to go open it and see what it is," she darted to the living room and I darted to the bathroom because I had to piss bad as hell.

While I was in the middle of relieving myself I flinched from hearing Zaria screaming at the top of her lungs. I cut the piss short, and dashed to the bedroom to grab my burner, and slowly made my way to the living room where I found Zaria standing by the front door still screaming with tears streaming down her face pointing at the package that was just delivered here.

I slowly approached the box, not knowing what to expect so I had to prepare myself for whatever it was. I looked inside the box and damn near jumped outta my own skin in fear. I gagged twice but prevented myself from vomiting all over the place. I glanced over at Zaria and she had stopped screaming but she was still crying and shaking. I slowly looked in the box again to make sure I wasn't hallucinating, but my eyes weren't playing tricks on me.

Inside the box was my nigga James little brother, Duke. His body was folded up like a pretzel, he was naked and bloody, but the thick plastic inside the box contained the blood from leaking out. I covered my nose, took a closer look and could see a big bullet hole at the top of his head. His forehead had the word R.E.D. carved across it in big letters. They did James lil brother grimy. Taped across his chest was a piece of paper, I hesitantly peeled it off his chest, and read it.

"But he who sins against me wrongs his own soul; All those that hate me love death'- Proverbs 8:36."

That nigga Slime was outta his fucking mind. The Red Mafiya done fucked up and killed the wrong person, and now shit done got real. These Muthafucka's sent a body through UPS, who does that?

"Zaria, go get dressed and pack up some clothes, we can't live here anymore," I instructed her, and she scurried to the bedroom still in shock.

I closed the box, and went to the bedroom to grab my phone. I wanted to call James to tell him about Duke, but I didn't want to be the one who delivered the fucked up news to him. Instead, I called my nigga Smurf and explained the situation to him and told him I needed him to clean up the mess and get rid of the body.

Chapter Nineteen

Gino

After Zaria packed up what she could, I took her to the Best Western hotel in Westland, which was located about twenty-five minutes outside of Detroit. I had her follow me in her car so she wouldn't be stuck in the hotel all day without transportation. Not that I really cared because I was on a mission to find out what was going on.

I didn't even wait until Smurf got to the condo to collect the body, but he just called to let me know that everything was taken care of. I was on my way back to the city to holla at Ace when I got an unexpected call from Mitch. He wanted to talk to me about some serious business, and suggested that we meet up face to face. I told him we can talk over the phone, but he insisted we meet up. I didn't know what type of shit he was on, but I didn't trust him one bit. I still decided to meet him, and told him to meet me at Northland Mall on 8 Mile and Greenfield. I chose a location where a lot of people would be present, and I had a number of routes to escape just in case I was being set up. Mitch always seemed shiesty to me, so he was most definitely a suspect.

I pulled into the somewhat packed mall parking lot, and parks as close as I could to the front entrance. I instructed Mitch to meet me at the food court, and he was already seated when I arrived. I checked out the scenery before I made my way to his table, and didn't see anything out of the ordinary.

"Mitch, what's the word nigga?" he stood up to give me dap, and a manly hug.

"I can't call it big homie. It's good to see you nigga, how you healing up?" he asked as we both took a seat at the small table.

"I'm as good as new. What's so important that we had to meet immediately?" I wasn't there for social hour so I cut straight to the chase. Mitch leaned forward in his chair, and rested his elbows on the table before he began to speak in a hushed tone.

"Gino, I know you don't really know me like that and you met me through yo brother, but I'm die hard loyal nigga. I got mad respect for you and the way you came home and took us to the next level. I'm 'bout that same thing," Mitch paused for a moment to look around, and then proceeded to talk. "I know I shouldn't be here telling you this, but if I see a flaw in our circle, I'm gone point it out and try to correct it. I'm coming to you because you the head of this whole operation, you the reason all this money flowing in so it's only right that I come to you if I see something that might jeopardize what we building."

"You said all that to say what?" I asked trying to get to the point.

"It's about Ace," he said, looking around again.

"What about him?" I asked getting real irritated.

"He has been on some bullshit lately. He hasn't been handling business right because he has been too high snorting that shit."

"Snorting that shit, what the fuck you talking about?" I asked in total disbelief.

"Oh, you ain't know? Ace snorting that white now! I stopped by his honeycomb the other day and he had some bitch up in there with him getting they nose dirty! I went over there to let him know the weight house on Gray Street was running low, and he in there partying with a table full of powder like he Rick James or something." He dramatically exclaimed, and then begins to look around again.

"Mitch what the fuck you keep looking around for?"

"I'm just watching my surroundings bro, that's all," he pleaded so I let the issue slide.

I know Ace ain't playing with his nose? What the fuck is running through his mind that he resorted to sniffing powder? I couldn't believe what Mitch was telling me, I know my brother wasn't breaking the code of the streets?

Just as I was about to say something to Mitch, I peeped a Mexican inside a store staring out of the glass window in my direction. I thought he would at least play it off and look in another direction, but he was staring directly at me and wanted me to know who he was. I looked at the store exactly across from the one and spotted two other Mexicans watching me too. I knew it probably were more hidden somewhere, but I didn't bother to continue to look around.

"Nigga you set me up?" I asked Mitch through clenched teeth.

"Set you up? What the fuck you mean set you up?" he asked, and I could see the fear in his eyes. I slid my hand under my shirt and gripped the handle of my pistol.

"Bitch nigga you set me up with the Mexicans?" I should blow yo muthafucking head off right now."

"What the fuck are you talking about? I don't know shit about no Mexicans, and I put it on my daughter I ain't got shit to do with setting you up." His words stumbled out of his mouth, and he started to panic but I believed him.

"Listen, it's some Mexicans watching us right now that-don't fucking look around." I nearly shrieked before he could fully turn his head around. "Don't fucking look at 'em just listen to me. They're here to kill me bro and I need you to help me get outta here alive. You got a banger on you?"

"Yeah-yeah I got one." He answered timidly.

"Good, be ready to shoot. We leaving that way over there," I discreetly pointed to my left. "When we stand up to leave, walk fast. If we make it outside, pull out yo pistol and follow me," before Mitch could protest, I stood up and he followed suit.

Before we made it ten steps to our designated exit, two Mexicans opened fire with two Tec 9's in the middle of the mall; I pulled out my gun but didn't know which way to aim.

Chapter Twenty

Slime

B aby, why you never let me have any fun?" asked Angelina.

"Because I'm saving you for something real special, it should be happening soon so be patient." I said while sitting on my red leather sofa doing a Sudoku puzzle to ease my mind.

I was at my four bedroom house in Sterling Heights I nicknamed, the Red House. Everything inside the house was completely red from the walls, carpet, and furniture, to the light bulbs, and dinnerware. I've been doing a lot of resting at the Red house, as well as strategizing.

I couldn't believe Gino thought he was smart enough to execute my demise. I knew Gino would send some amateurs instead of some certified professionals. Since I knew what to expect, I capitalized off the hit like any great thinker would.

I waited a week before I used my enemy-which was Gino-to kill my other enemy, which was Zeek.

Zeek was one of my workers who had the duty of picking up, and transporting money for the Red Mafiya. But Zeek did the ultimate betrayal: he stole money and lied about it when confronted. So when the time was right I sent Zeek to pick up a "package" for me on the eastside and let him drive my corvette. And just as I expected, Gino inexperience henchmen sported the Vette, thought it was me behind the wheel, and riddled the car with bullets.

I knew about Gino bringing those Flint niggas to Detroit, and I had my people watching their every move. After those Flint flunkies killed Zeek, two of my certified killas kidnapped one of the lil bitches, and tortured him for hours then shipped him to Gino's Riverfront condo so he would know he could get touched at any time.

I could easily kill Gino, Ace and they whole squad but I rather see them sweat. I loved to mentally torture my enemies more than anything. But to be honest, I didn't really want to kill Gino. I felt sorry for Gino because he got fresh outta the joint and inherited his illiterate brother's problems, not even knowing his brother was the enemy.

"Baby, you told me that same thing a month ago," said Angelina in a whining voice.

Angelina is a Red Mafiya Bloodette who thrived off killing. Anybody I ordered her to kill she doesn't think twice before getting the job done. So far she had twenty-three bodies under her belt, and was thirsty for more blood. But you would never know Angelina was an assassin by looking at her. She was 5'6, 130 pounds, emerald green eyes, curvaceous, long hair, full blooded Italian. She resembled an innocent college student but was absolutely the opposite.

"I know what I told you. Everything unfolding as we speak boo boo. Once the time is right, I'll send you to clean up the mess. Patience is a virtue," I finally completed the Sudoku puzzle, and then smiled to myself.

Chapter Twenty-One

Gino

While I was contemplating on which way to shoot, Mitch surprised me by pulling out two lemon squeeze P89 Rugers, and start blazing with glory! I started shooting in the opposite direction of him, so we ended up back to back side stepping our way to the nearest exit.

It seemed like bullets were coming from everywhere but only missing us by inches. I spotted several mall cops approach us with guns, and knew we had to make a quick getaway before the real authorities showed up.

"We gotta hurry up and get the fuck on." I yelled over the screams of pedestrians, and the echoes of the weapons being fired.

I fired a few more shots and I wish I would've waited just a few more seconds before doing so because one of my bullets went into the chest of a young girl that looked no more than 12 years old. When I seen her little body drop to the waxed tile floor, it felt like my heart dropped at the same precise time. I just ended a precious innocent life with no valid justification no matter how many I came up with in that short time period. I stood there froze in the line of fire staring at the little girl until

Mitch grabbed my arm and yanked me as he dashed towards the exit. I glanced back one last time, and whispered I'm sorry to the soul floating above the lifeless body, and then caught up with fleeing Mitch.

We finally made it outside but that wasn't a celebration moment because the Mexicans were right behind us still shooting. It was like they had an unlimited supply of fucking bullets in their pockets. I led the way as we scrambled to my truck, turning around every few feet to return fire. Mitch covered me as I grabbed the keys out of my pocket to hit the alarm, but just as I was about to get in and take off, something came to me.

"Aye Mitch, duck down and get to the back of the truck. Come on nigga." He followed my orders and eased his way to the back of the truck.

I hit a button on the keypad, and the back door came up. I hurriedly grabbed the AR-15 that I almost forgot I put in there while I was moving Zaria to Westland. I knew it was already loaded and ready to shoot so I wasted no time aiming and opening fire. Just as I expected, the Mexicans hit the asphalt in a split second. I let off at least thirty shots before Mitch and I jumped in the Trailblazer. Once I got it started, I pulled off burning rubber in the process.

Chapter Twenty-Two

Mitch

"M itch, you're not giving us enough information to nail these fuckers to the cross."

"How much more information do you need, I gave you all that you need to fry Ace, and Gino." I replied in an aggravated tone. I was tired of reporting to Agent Graham, it seemed like it was taking forever for this pink bitch to issue warrants on Ace and Gino.

I became an informant for the FBI over three months ago after I got caught with them twenty bricks of white on my way back from Houston. At first I stood strong like a real soldier, but once I started thinking about being away from my daughter for 30 years, I decided to switch sides to avoid all jail time. So for the last three months I've been giving the feds info on the two leaders of the group which was Ace, and Gino. Truth be told, I supplied them with enough info to prosecute them muthafucka's when I turned over the tape of the club shooting. But once the feds discovered Slime was at war with Ace, they wanted to get some evidence on Slime, who they have been investigating for a year, to put him away for a long time too. They were just waiting for him to slip up.

"I need you to get close enough to Gino, that he trusts you enough to let you have his dick hairs. Gino is the one that does all the communicating with Slime, so get buddy buddy with him before either of them end up dead. I need Slime's head on the chopping block along with your comrades." yelled Agent Graham. They were sitting in Agent Graham's unmarked police car in the Bel Air shopping center parking lot.

"I'm working on it right now-"

"How, by shooting up malls, and killing innocent freaking kids, for Christ sake." He emphasized by throwing his hands in the air. "If the local police figure out your involved, I'm not saving your ass this time. Now do what I said and bring me all three of them in a box with a pretty little ribbon around it, or that's your ass. Get the fuck outta my car." I didn't even reply, I just did as he said.

I thought about how bad it was and how I got myself into this predicament in the first place. Being a rat was hard work, harder than I ever thought it would be, but I had to get the job done by any means. My freedom depended on it.

Chapter Twenty-Three

Gino

L o-Lo funeral was earlier today, but I didn't bother to attend for a number of reasons. For one, I knew the homicide detectives would be swarming the place looking for any possible suspect to interrogate, and I didn't have time for the hassle. For two, the Mexican Mafia, and I'm pretty sure the Red Mafiya were expecting me to show up, but if they thought I was that stupid, then there were absolutely wrong. For three, Lo-Lo did the unthinkable by betraying me so I could give two fucks about attending his service. I paid for it out of respect for his family, and I had to make it seem like he was still my dog in front of Nadia, or she would've knew something was up.

Since I didn't attend the funeral, I figured I should at least visit Nadia so I was on my way to her apartment. I had to trade in the Trailblazer rental after the shooting incident at the mall, now I was driving a 2004 Acura. I couldn't believe that I escaped the shootout alive after the news reported that they gathered an estimate of four hundred shell cases. They had video footage on every local news station, and even on the major news stations such as CNN, FOX News, and HLN. The only thing that hindered them from making an arrest was the resolution of the video was too horrible to identify who was involved.

I barely got any sleep last night; I was too busy thinking about the little girl that lost her life in the mayhem. And it didn't help that the news stations had her picture, and the story of her short lived life plastered on almost every channel. Jesse Jackson and Al Sharpton even came to Detroit to hold a news conference, and show the family some form of support.

Her name was Jasmine Appletree, a 12 year old honor student that spent her free time playing tennis. Her family said that she could've been the next Serena Williams, but they will never know how successful she may have been because of a senseless shooting. I planned to send her family a nice amount of money in the form of a donation, that's the least I could do.

I had a new found respect for Mitch; he handled that situation like a true soldier. All the doubts of loyalty, him being too timid, vanished yesterday, when he showed me what he was about. I definitely planned to keep him on my team because it was hard to find a solid nigga now days. Most of these niggaz were rats, snakes, or straight up cowards. Now that he proved that he was neither, I had nothing but loyalty for him. And then after what he told me about Ace, I had to go have a talk with him today. I was hoping that it wasn't true, but if it was then I couldn't fuck with Ace on the business aspect anymore. I mean, I loved my brother but his downfall won't bring me down.

I pulled up and parked in front of Nadia's apartment building at almost 8 o'clock at night, and the sky was clear with a cool breeze blowing. I had two Glock .40 calibers on me today and an AK-47 in the trunk. I was well prepared this time if any surprises arose.

When I got to Nadia's door, she opened it wearing a long t-shirt so I couldn't tell if she had anything on underneath it. I could look at her and tell she had been crying because her eyes were still puffy. I stepped through the threshold and gave her a firm hug, then a kiss on the lips.

"I missed you baby girl," I whispered in her ear.

"I missed you too, Gino. I wish you would've came to the funeral, I needed somebody to hold me," I released her from my embrace, and then she closed and locked the door.

I took a seat on the couch and she sat next to me with a smug look on her face. I hated that she had to suffer for her cousin's mishaps, but I had to kill the nigga and I didn't regret it one bit. Some shit you just couldn't let slide no matter how much love you have for that individual. I still had love for Lo-Lo even after what he did to Autumn, but he paid for it with his manhood while he was still alive, and then with his life after I felt he was tortured enough. But it was innocent people like Nadia who were also affected by the lost, and she didn't deserve that.

228

"I told you I couldn't see my nigga like that," I replied showing some type of emotion.

"But it was a closed casket," she quickly pointed out.

"And that made it even worse, I couldn't do it baby. I just buried my little sister; I couldn't watch my nigga be buried in the same month.

"I understand baby, I'm not mad at you," said Nadia, buying my excuse. "Who was that girl you had drop that money off to me?" she asked raising her right eyebrow.

"That was a friend, she be running errands for me when I tell her to," Nadia gave me a 'nigga please!' look, and then rolled her eyes.

"What's all that for?"

"Because you're not very good at lying, but it doesn't matter because she can't do it like me."

"Do what like you? I asked but knowing what she was referring to.

"Do this…," Nadia stood up in front of me, and took off her t-shirt exposing her firm titties, and wasted no time pulling down her pink boy shorts and kicking them to the side.

I knew what time is was, so I removed the two Glocks from my waist, and placed them on the coffee table. I would enjoy myself tonight because after today I couldn't fuck with Nadia anymore. I wanted to be loyal to Destiny like she was loyal to me. I planned to give Nadia the fuck of her life, and then I'll walk out of it for good. She deserved a better man anyway.

After three hours of licking, sucking, kissing, and fucking, we laid there in the bed together sweaty and exhausted. She knew exactly how to please a man as if she was an experienced 40 year old woman. But to my dismay, I had to break the bad news to her. I peeked over at her and she had her eyes shut breathing lightly like she was dozing off.

"Nadia…," I whispered.

"Huh…?" she answered slightly opening her eyes. She looked so sexy and angelic.

"I gotta tell you something," I could tell that I got her full attention because she opened her eyes all the way, and looked at me.

"Tell me what?" she asked with an obvious inquiring mind. I paused to take a deep breath, and figure out how I was going to tell her without upsetting her.

"Let me start off by saying that I got a lot of love for you, Nadia. I really do, and I don't want you to ever forget that," I could see the uneasiness in her facial expression.

"Why are you telling me all this?"

"I'll tell you this because after today… I can't see you anymore, "and just as I expected Nadia flipped the script as she sat straight up in the bed.

"What do you mean you can't see me anymore? Where is all this coming from?" the questions didn't make it any easier for me or her, but come to think of it there is no easy way to leave a female unexpectedly. I sat up in the bed too just in case she decided to do something crazy.

"Calm down baby-"

"Calm down my ass! Explain to me why you can't see me anymore. I need an explanation Gino."

"Listen I'm moving outta Michigan within a week, so it's time for you to move on with your life too," I explained, but only telling her what I wanted her to know.

"I don't care if you move to Bohemia, I'm coming with you!"

"No you're not," I calmly replied.

"Yes I am!" she shouted back, and I didn't know what to say to calm her down.

"Nadia…," I gave her a stern look. "You're not coming with me."

"Why…? Why can't I come, Gino? Huh…? Please tell me why?" she was becoming delirious.

"Because I said you can't, that's why," I simply responded, and then Nadia got up from the bed still ass naked, and rested her hands on her hips.

"So it's another bitch huh?" she finally asked.

"That don't matter so we not gone even discuss that," I got outta the bed and begin to get dresses.

"So that's what it is, Gino? You can't be a man and tell me the truth? You supposed to be such a real nigga so keep it real. You found you another bitch, probably that bitch you had bring me that money, then said, fuck my feelings?" She stung my heart, and then the fresh tears streaming down her face didn't' make it any better.

Once I had my pants all the way on, I walked over to her and tried to console her but she pushed me away. I stood there and felt bad I couldn't take her with me. I couldn't betray Destiny no matter how bad I felt about breaking her heart.

"Don't fucking touch me! I hate your fucking guts nigga." She screamed at the top of her lungs.

I walked back over to the other side of the bed, and continued to get dressed. Once I was fully dressed, I pulled out a roll of money which was over ten grand and threw it on the bed. I looked at Nadia and she just stood there hugging herself as she shook involuntarily.

"Please...don't... leave me... please," she stammered, and I wanted to drop some tears my damn self, but I had to remain calm for the both of us.

"I love you Nadia... if you ever need anything...call me," I walked outta the bedroom door into the living room, grabbed my two pistols off the coffee table, and I could still hear her weeping as I walked outta the front door.

Chapter Twenty-Four

Gino

The next day I didn't really feel like being bothered, so I chilled at Destiny's house most of the day. Zaria had to work, so that allowed me to spend time with my future wifey. I had intentions of popping up on Ace, but all that was put aside when I got a call from Slime. He wanted me to meet him at a church we attended frequently when we were young on Wade and Hayes.

At first I declined his offer because I didn't know if it was a set up or not. He stressed that he wouldn't disrespect neutral territory, but I thought about how he had Autumn snatched up and I couldn't believe shit he said. He swore on his flag he wasn't on any set up shit so I agreed to meet him, Chances make champions, and I was taking a hell of a chance.

I wondered why he wanted to meet with me in the first place, especially after I tried to have him murdered. I was praying it was some type of peace treaty, because I was sick of watching my back and running for my life. Sooner or later I won't be so lucky, and it'll be goodnight for me. Just as I was getting off the freeway my cell phone begins to ring and it was Murda.

"What up my nigga?" I answered

"What it is fam? Where the fuck you at?" he asked sounding concerned.

"I'm on the eastside. Why you ask that?"

"Nigga you don't know that somebody kicked in yo door and shot up the safe house on W. Boston?"

"Hell nawl I ain't know. I ain't slid through there in a few days," I replied surprised that the house was shot up.

"Yeah bro, I was about to drop some bags off there, and when I pulled up I looked at the house and got the fuck on. The front door was wide open, all the windows in the front were shattered, and bullet holes redecorated that muthafucka."

"That's crazy." Was all I could say?

"Yeah I know, who you think did that shit? I'm ready for whatever bro, just give me a name!" I thought about who would do some petty shit like that, and the first person I could think of was James, but I wasn't sure.

"I don't know bro, but I'll investigate it. I'm glad I didn't have any money in that bitch." I said, relieved that I moved the money to Destiny's house.

"Hell yeah. Where you want me to take this money?"

"Hold on to it for me my nigga. Call Smurf and tell him not to take my cuts over there, just hold on to it until I get back with y'all," I had just pulled up to the church.

"Alright, I got u my dude. Hit me up if you need me, I'm here for u my nigga."

"I appreciate that my nigga, I'll get at you later," I hung up the phone knowing I had a loyal friend in Murda.

I looked at the big church, and I didn't know what to expect once I step foot out of this car. I thought about how Slime, Ace and I used to come to this church to get some girls to leave church with us. You know what they say, church girls are the freakiest and I was a testament to that. I wish I could go back to those days when life was simpler. Got me thinking life was better when I was dead broke.

I finally got outta the Acura, and took in my surroundings. There wasn't one car parked in front of the church, they must've parked around back. I stood tall as I walked up the long walkway leading to the stairs, and the front entrance. Once I climbed the stairs, and walked through the big wooden double doors, I was greeted by two huge niggas holding Heckler & Koch assault rifles with clips longer than my whole arm. They nodded towards the doors leading to the sanctuary, and I followed their silent instructions.

I see Slime sitting on a pew in the middle of the sanctuary with his head down as if he was praying; I slowly walked toward him and looked around at the same time. I turned around and looked up towards the balcony to find four more huge niggas with the HK's looking down on me. These niggas ain't have no respect for the church with weapons all out in the open. But who was I to judge when I had two Glocks on my waist, could never be too careful. I turned back around to find Slime standing behind me with a dominate look on his face.

"Gino, let's take a seat my nigga, I got some valuable Intel you might be happy to receive," said Slime gesturing I take a seat so I stepped into the pew, and sat down. I noticed a manila envelope sitting on the pew, so I picked it up.

"What's in here?" I asked without opening it.

"I'll show you in a minute, first let's talk," he replied in a calm manner, and I had the feeling he was about to tell me something that would alter my life.

"I usually don't be too cordial to niggas who attempted to take my life-"

"Listen Slime, man I swear-"I started to protest but he lifted his left hand to silence me.

"I'm not here for excuses my nigga, I already chalked that shit up to you being in distress over the loss of Autumn. Just don't try that fuck shit again," my heart was beating rapidly as Slime talked, and I didn't know if Slime forgiving me was sincere or not, I just wanted to get the fuck outta that church.

"I'm not going to retaliate," he continued. "I'm here to express the truth, and offer an option to you. I just need to know are you willing to compromise?" he asked finally looking me in the eyes. I diverted my attention to the pulpit, and came up with the assumption that I didn't have much of a choice.

"Yeah, we can compromise as long as it's a suitable agreement."

"Good, I'm going to start off with your brother's homie Mitch," I looked back at Slime, and sat up straight when he mentioned Mitch's name. He had my full attention. What did Mitch have to do with anything?'

"That nigga Mitch is a federal informant," he announced in a nonchalant manner.

"What! Get the fuck outta here." I said in complete shock.

Slime reached over and grabbed the envelope out of my hand, and discreetly leafed through the contents inside it. He pulled out over ten photos and handed them to me. I carefully looked over the pictures and thought my eyes were playing tricks on me. In one picture Mitch was holding a conversation with what I assumed was a federal agent in an unmarked vehicle. I shifted through the other photos and came across a face sheet of the man in the other pictures with Mitch, on the face sheet it displayed everything I wanted to know, the man name was Agent Graham and he was a 10 year FBI veteran.

"How long he been a rat?" I asked.

"He's been eating cheese for over three months. My source told me he was on his way back from Houston with twenty bricks of ya yo, and the state troopers flicked him. They released him once he folded and agreed to help build a case on you and your brother. Well, that was the initial agreement, but shit done got complicated."

"How so?"

"My name is involved in the investigation now because of the ongoing feud between us. My name steady popping up and now they want me on the same indictment list as you. But that's not likely to happen because I'm ten steps ahead of them bitches," he said with much confidence.

I couldn't believe what he had just revealed to me. Mitch was a fucking rat. Just when I thought he was a stand-up nigga, I find out he working the feds. How worse could it get for me?'

"Does Mel know about it?" I asked.

"Nawl, don't nobody know but us."

"So what's in it for you because I know you're not telling me all this for nothing?" I asked knowing he had his own ulterior motive behind telling me.

"I'll tell you what I want after I tell you everything you need to know about past and current events," he said giving me a look I couldn't analyze.

"What you mean past and current events?"

"This is what I'm talking about right here," he reached into the envelope again and pulled out some more pictures and handed them to me.

The first picture I looked at hit me hard, my heart wanted to jump out of my chest and kill itself. I could feel my eyes fill up with tears, but I couldn't release them. Not in front of Slime, I had to be strong in front of him for the sake of pride.

"Where you get these from?" I asked with my voice cracking a little bit.

"I had my people take pictures a while ago. Once I found out that Ace was the one that robbed Birdie. I had my peoples watch his movements. They watched his every move, knew all his stash houses, and safe houses, weight houses, and they even knew where he rested his head at. All they had to do was follow him and he led them straight to Zaria house one rainy night. You know I've been knowing Zaria since she first started being your girlfriend, so once I found out he was fucking with her, I knew he had no sense of loyalty. That's the main reason I charged him that much money for robbing Birdie, he was a snake in the grass. And once you came home I couldn't go back on my demand because I had no respect for that nigga no matter if he didn't know he was taking from me or not. Not only was he banging your bitch while you were in the can, but he still fucking her since you've been home!" he shook his head in disgust, and I didn't know what to feel.

The discovery was breaking my heart piece by piece. It seemed that everybody I loved was betraying me while I was giving them undying, loyalty. Now everything was coming together and a lot of shit started to make sense. The Red Mafiya came to Zaria's house to kidnap Ace because he was always over there fucking her behind my back. And Zaria had been coming in late because she was with Ace who probable had her sniffing coke too. Why couldn't I figure all this out before now? Probably because I never would've imagined Ace would do some hoe shit like this.

"Yeah, fucked up ain't it?" Slime said with a hint of remorse. "So now that you know how much of a snake Ace is, I'm about to tell you the worse of it all."

"What the fuck you mean?" I asked trying to figure out what could be worse that the news I already learned?

Slime once again reached inside the manila envelope and removed the remaining pictures, and scanned them over himself before passing them to me. I forced myself to look at the first photo and was confused at first. When I got to the second photo a sharp pain covered my whole chest, and I didn't even realize I was holding my breath. This shit couldn't be true.

The second picture was captured outside of some warehouse of Ace, and the man that looked me in the eyes before he riddled me with bullets, Lucky. They were embracing each other in a friendly manner, and it was taken a few days ago according to the date printed on the corner of the picture. I leafed through the rest of the pictures, and I could feel my heart turn black. All along the enemy was right in my face.

Poncho told me, vivora en el sacate desde la cuana, and he was absolutely accurate. What he told me was it was 'Snakes in the grass from the cradle'. I overlooked Ace because he was my brother. Everything made perfect sense, and Ace was the cause of everything. Ace was the one who told Lucky I robbed and killed Mook, but why? Was it envy, Jealousy, greed or money…?" Why would my own brother want me dead? How could he sleep at night knowing he's trying to cover up his guilt? But why didn't he just send the Mexican Mafia to my condo where he could've easily had me murdered…? ZARIA!! Zaria was the reason he didn't send them to the condo. He knew if Zaria was there when they showed up, she would've been killed too. He wanted to protect Zaria, and my head started to spin. Slime just gave me all the info I was searching for at one time, and to be honest I wish I didn't know the truth. I finally stopped staring and the pictures, and looked at Slime.

"Slime, please tell me these pictures were photo shopped?" I practically begged.

"I wish they were my baby, I wish they were," he somberly replied as he stood up. "But since they ain't, infidelity results in death. Take care of Mitch ASAP and I'll take care of Ace for you. You shouldn't have to live with killing your lil brother on your conscience. It's all on you if you want to confront Ace or not, but I want to do you that favor by getting rid of him," I could tell he already had his mind made up, and it wasn't up for debate.

"So where do we stand," I asked for clarification.

"As long as you get rid of Mitch, we stand on common ground. You go your way, I'll go mine, noting in between."

"That's your word?" he responded hold his right hand up to his heart.

At that moment I knew the beef between me and the Red Mafiya was over, but I still had a war going on with the Mexican Mafia, and my own brother. Lord, protect me from my friends because I can handle my enemies.

Chapter Twenty-Five

Nadia

"I Fucking hate him." I picked up a glass vase and threw it at the wall, glass shattered everywhere into tiny pieces.

I had been deeply depressed since Gino told me he couldn't see me again. I locked myself in my room for the past couple of days and cried my eyes dry. I didn't attend any of my classes, answer my phone, and barely ate or slept. No matter how hard I tried, I just couldn't imagine living without him, I just couldn't. I tried to think rationale but I couldn't grasp the idea of moving on with my life. Gino was all I had and all I ever wanted since I was young and for him to walk outta my life without a legit explanation crushed my soul.

I was positive he stopped fucking with me because of another bitch, and the only bitch that came to my mind was the bitch he had bring me that money for Lo-Lo's funeral. I would bet a million dollars that she was the reason he cut me off, I wish I knew where the bitch stayed. I would race over there and beat that bitch senseless. How could he do this to me? How could he use me like an old rag doll, and throw me to the side? If I couldn't have him then no bitch would.

I grabbed my phone from the nightstand and begin to dial quickly. I waited patiently until someone answered, and then cleared my throat before I spoke.

"This is 911, what is your emergency?" asked the operator.

"I would like to speak with whoever is in charge with the DEA office; I have some valuable information that could get a drug kingpin off the streets."

"Okay I'll connect you to the DEA office, ma'am." I heard the phone click, and I was put on hold.

If I couldn't have him, nobody would.

Chapter Twenty-Six

Gino

O ur relationships with other people are subject to the characteristic of impermanence and change. Friends become enemies; enemies become friends; even enemies become close relatives; while relatives become enemies.

Words couldn't formulate the agony my heart was enduring since Slime provided me with the information I was looking for two days ago. It was arduous to accept the fact that Zaria cheated on me with my own brother. I couldn't cope with Ace trying to have Lucky kill me, I wasn't even mad about it, I was more hurt than anything…he hurt me bad. I guess love and loyalty didn't exist whenever the root of all evil was money.

And to make matters worse, the fucking feds were watching me. I knew it was something suspicious about Mitch, I always had that feeling. How much the feds knew about me; I didn't have a clue. But one thing I did know was that he had to be eliminated immediately.

Since the meeting at the church with Slime, I've been staying at Destiny's house. I turned my phone off and stayed in the bed most of the

246

day, I had to get my mind together and let my soul rest. Destiny was worried about me, and insisted that I talk about what was on my mind. As bad as I wanted to I couldn't tell her the situation. The less she knew the better off she was.

With everything that was going on I still was grieving over the loss of Autumn. I missed my little sister every day, and the pain wouldn't subside. She was dragged into this war for no apparent reason, and no matter what she was gone forever. I guess it was all a part of the game I'm was playing.

I couldn't stay ducked off in this house forever, I had to make some moves to tie up these loose ends. Before I did anything I needed to go to the cemetery to visit Autumn, because it may be the last time I visit her for a while.

Destiny was at her Real Estate class at the moment so I had to handle my business before she came home. She's been there for me the best way she knew how for the past couple of days, and I plan on showing her my gratitude for the rest of my life. I snatched up my phone from off the bed, and turned it on after two whole days and was greeted by a full voicemail. I didn't have time to listen to messages, I had my own agenda right now and I didn't need any distractions. The first person I called was Smurf.

"What it is my dude?" where you been hiding at, I been trying to hit you up?" asked Smurf.

"What's good my baby, I been laying low putting this plan together. How's business doing?"

"Everything good on the dog food, but that white girl 'bout to stop running in a minute. Is everything good with you?"

"Right now I'm straight. Ain't any shorts on what you sitting on for me, everything counted for?" I asked referring to my percentage of money I had Smurf hold for me.

"Everything counted for, ain't no shorts or nothing," he replied.

"Alright cool. Listen, I'm gone call yo back in a couple of hours my nigga. What I need you to do right now it shut down all the spots temporarily. Call up Murda and tell him I need him in the city right away, and I'm gone need y'all to put some work in. Make sure y'all are ready for me to call back in a couple hours, understood?"

"Yeah bro, I'm 'bout to hit up Murda right now and shut down everything. Make sure you call me back bro, we ready for whatever," he assured me and I was relieved to know I could still depend on them if I couldn't depend on nobody else.

"Alright, one my nigga."

"One," he responded before hanging up.

Today's weather was perfect for the occasion for the way I was feeling; cold and gloomy. The breeze from the wind was bone chilling, and the clouds were almost as dark as my heart and seemed on the brinks of a rainstorm. I parked the Acura on the cub close to Autumn's headstone, and grabbed the flowers off the passenger seat that I picked up from the floral shop on Conner's Ave. I decided to get a dozen white roses that symbolized purity, because my sister was the pure side of me that will never return.

The grass was covered in mist but that didn't stop me from taking a seat in front of her grave. I placed the white roses on top of the headstone, and begin to trace her name on the tomb with my index finger.

"What up lil sis?" I knew she couldn't hear me, but I found relief in pretending she could.

"I'm sorry baby girl… I swear I'm sorry. I wish like hell you were still here… you didn't deserve this," I had to pause to control my emotions that I didn't want to escape. "I wish I could turn back the hands of time… I love you baby girl. I love you so much that it hurts…if I could trade places with you, I'll do it in a heartbeat-"

"Me too," said a voice behind me, and I didn't even have to turn around to recognize the voice. I continued to stare at the headstone to control my rage.

"Why haven't you been answering your phone?" asked Ace.

I finally stood up to turn around and face Ace, and he looked disheveled and exhausted. His nose was dripping with snot, he had dark circles around his eyes, and despite the cold weather he still wore shorts and a t-shirt. Looking into his eyes I could see the change in Ace, he wasn't himself and the drugs was making it worse.

"I been getting my mind right, and laying low. How did you know I was here?"

"I didn't," he simply replied while wiping his nose with the back of his hand. "Why are you avoiding me, Gino? Ain't I your brother?" he asked swaying back and forth, and the question caught me completely off guard.

I wonder if he knew I found out about his betrayal. Did he know that I knew about him and Zaria, and that he was trying to have me killed? I doubt it very much; I think he was too high to even suspect such a thing. The rain was starting to pick up so his t-shirt was soaking wet sticking to him, and I could see the imprint of a pistol on his waistline.

"I should be asking you the same question. What changed between us?" I asked.

"I don't know…," was all he could manage to whisper.

"I know what's been going on, Ace. I know everything," I paused to look Ace in the eyes but he put his head down, his chin resting on his chest. "I know about Zaria…out of all the women in the world why her?" no answer, he just stood there with his head down.

"And then you told Lucky I robbed and killed Mook. You tried to have me killed. I'm your fucking brother nigga; we got the same blood flowing through our veins. These streets made you that ruthless? What was it…money-"

"It ain't never been about no fucking money!" he yelled cutting my sentence short.

"So what's it about, Ace?" I asked again trying my hardest to fight back tears. It was raining heavy now and everything I had on was becoming drenched.

"It was you Gino. You came home trying to call shots and looking down on me as if I would be nothing without you. I made this shit happen not you, ME! But you never acknowledged that, you had to be the one who called all the shots, didn't you? Then it was your mans that raped Autumn. Lo-Lo the reason our little sister is dead. But you overlooked all your faults… and quick to point mines out," even though it was raining you could still see his teardrops sliding down his cheeks.

"So what's your excuse for fucking my girl while I was in the joint?" You fucking my main bitch behind my back, what part of the game is that!?!"

"Zaria pursued me. She put my dick in her mouth. She ain't shit but a gold-digging slut bitch, that's your fault for falling in love with that hoe." I couldn't even get mad at Ace's comments because I knew his definition of loyalty was different from mine.

"So what you gone do now? Kill me?" You gone do me that favor by burying me next to Autumn? You gone kill your little brother, your only brother?" Ace asked sobbing dramatically.

I couldn't kill Ace if my life depended on it; I still loved him with all my heart. I couldn't squeeze the trigger myself, but I already made a deal with Slime. Ace was living on borrowed time and he didn't even know it. This was without a doubt the last time I would see my little brother alive. That thought alone caused me to choke up.

I slowly walked over to him, stared at him for minute, and I could see the regret in his eyes. I could see the brother I knew before I went to prison in his eyes, the loyal brother. The brother that I would kill or die for without second guessing. But looks can be deceiving, and it was too late for remorse.

I reached out and hugged Ace as tight as I could while he cried on my shoulder. I kissed him on the forehead, let him go, and walked away. Blood is thicker than water, but loyalty will always be thicker than blood. Infidelity is a contagious virus to individuals with a weak loyalty immune system; therefore I was vaccinated at birth. I thought Ace was too… but I was so wrong. Damn Ace… I still love you lil bro… I always will.

Chapter Twenty-Seven

Gino

After leaving ace at the cemetery, I called up Smurf and told him and Murda to meet me at Belle Isle Park. Zaria and Nadia had been calling my phone nonstop since I turned it back on. I ignored Nadia calls because I didn't have time to argue with her, but I did text Zaria back to let her know I was okay, and I was on my way to see her in a few hours.

When I got to Belle Isle, both of my niggas was already there parked near the river. The rain had slowed up and it was coming down in a drizzle. I parked next to Smurf's Yukon, got outta my car and left it running, then got in the backseat of his truck.

"I wanted to meet up with y'all to discuss some fucked up news. I need y'all assistance in a major way; it's some fucked up shit in the game. If y'all not trying to get y'all hands dirty then let me know, it won't be no hard feelings," I looked at both of my first two real niggas I considered my friends to see any sign of weakness. Murda turned around in his seat to face me.

"You know I'm riding to the end, my baby. I don't see why you would ask such a question," he said showing me where his loyalty is.

"I'm down for whatever my nigga, just give me the word and I'm squeezing!" replied Smurf.

Knowing I was gone receive the response that they gave me, I begin to tell them that Mitch was an informant for the feds. They were just as surprised as I was at the discovery, but the surprise quickly turned into hatred. I begin to tell them the plan to get the nigga without being seen.

"So I'm gone call the nigga and tell him to meet me at the weight house we got ducked off on Park Grove Street so I can smash some bricks on him. Right now he thinks we rocking with each other because of the shootout we had with them wetbacks at the mall-"

"That was y'all niggas" asked Murda.

"Hell yeah, them bitches tried to take my head off. But anyways, since he thinks we still cool, I'm gone use that to my advantage to lure him over there. Once he get there instead of me answering the door, one of y'all niggas gone answer it. Once you get him in the house, and lock the door, tell the nigga I'm in the basement waiting on him. When he gets down the steps y'all can handle y'all business. I'm not even gone be there because I got some shit I need to tend too, but I'm sure y'all niggas can handle that fuck nigga," I explained.

"So we gotta play like you in the basement, once he gets in the basement kill him?" asked Smurf making sure he understood the plan.

"Exactly, but make sure just one of y'all answer the door, and the other one wait in the basement. We don't want this nigga to get paranoid," I stressed.

"So when you gone call this nigga?" asked Murda.

"Right now," I pulled my phone from my pocket and dialed Mitch number and he answered after the second ring.

"What up doe, Gino?"

"What up my nigga, what you got going on?"

"Not a damn thing, trying to get money," he replied.

"That's what I like to hear. But peep this my nigga, I need you to slide over here on Park grove to pick up and take these white girls to yo location. You know where I'm talking 'bout?"

"Yeah I know exactly where you at. When you want me to slide through there?" he asked eagerly.

"Gimme 'bout an hour," I instructed him.

"I'll be there my nigga," and then we ended the call.

"Now that that's outta the way, y'all niggas head over there, here go the key," I took the key off my key ring and gave it to Murda.

"This shit gone be a piece of cake, we'll hit you up when everything squared away," said Smurf.

"That's what I like to hear, y'all boys be careful."

"Before you leave, grab them two bags outta the back. That's the money we been holding for you. Its 3.5 million altogether," Smurf enlightened me.

"Good looking out my niggas. I got something for y'all when the job is completed, so make sure you hit me up," I grabbed the two duffel bags outta the back, and exited the truck.

After dropping the duffel bags off at Destiny's house and convincing her that I'll be right back, I got on the freeway and was on my way to Westland to see Zaria. Carl Thomas hit song 'Emotional' was on repeat blaring through the speakers as I drove above the speed limit.

All the shit we built together, and been through together meant absolutely nothing to her obviously. I mean, sure I cheated on her before, but I would never disrespect her by fucking her sister, cousin, friend or anybody close to her. It's a certain line we as men never cross when it comes to our woman. So for her to fuck my brother while I was in prison was disloyalty at an all-time high. Forgiveness was outta the question, she was dead to me.

Instead of parking in the lot of the hotel, I decided to park around the corner on a residential street. I walked around the block and entered the hotel entrance with my Al Wissam hood over my head. Instead of using the elevator I took the stairs until I reached the fifth floor. I opened the stairwell door and peeked down the hallway, making sure both sides were clear. I reached in my pocket and fished out the card-key to my room, and then dashed down the hallway making sure I was concealed by the hood. I swiftly swiped the card, opened and closed the door behind me, and then took a long deep breath. The sound of the shower running told me Zaria was either still in the shower or in the bedroom.

I looked around the living area and everything was tidy and neat. I eased my way to the kitchen and picked up a chopping knife off the countertop, and slid it up my sleeve. I then went back to the living room area and took a seat on the sofa to wait for Zaria. After waiting for twenty minutes she finally emerged from the back room with nothing on but a towel wrapped around her.

"Oh my God, Gino! You scared the shit outta me." She said holding her heart. I didn't even say anything; I just gave her a blank stare. "What's the matter baby, why haven't I seen you in two days?" She asked sitting down next to me wrapping her arms around my neck, and kissing me on the lips. She removed the hood from my head, and looked at me with confusion.

"I just have been stressing lately trying to find out how my life became so hectic. Maybe you could help me figure that out." She had an even more confused look on her face, not understanding what I was insinuating.

"I don't know what you're asking me, baby. You're not telling me what's going on."

"You really think I'm stupid, don't you?"

"What are you talking about?"

"You think I'm dumb, don't you?" I asked again becoming angrier.

"Gino, what are you talking about!?!" she pleaded as she removed her arms from around my neck.

"Bitch you snorting coke, and fucking my brother, and now you wanna play innocent." I screamed as I watched her eyes begin to bulge.

"Who told you that Gino? I swear to-"

"Bitch you bet not lie to me. I know what it is and what it's been, I got the fucking proof." I reached into my jacket pocket and pulled out the picture of her and Ace together that I got from Slime.

She looked at the pictures and stood up from the couch with a frightened look on her face. She stood there speechless, didn't know what to say now that I knew the truth.

259

"You ain't got shit to say now, huh...?"

"I'm so sorry, Gino. I didn't mean to hurt you baby, I was just lonely and I-"

"Felt that my brother dick could comfort you, is that what it was? Did you know how much I loved you, Zaria? Did you know I was out here sacrificing my life and freedom so you could live without worry? Did you know I would've killed and died for you?" I whispered more to myself that Zaria.

"I'm...sorry," was all she could say as she wailed.

"Yeah, I know... you're sorry. Me too, Zaria... I'm sorry too," I got up and went to the bedroom to check and make sure no one was there. You never knew if she had a nigga here or not.

On the night stand next to the bed was a small amount of cocaine. I shook my head in disgust and then walked back to the front room where Zaria was sitting on the couch still crying. I grabbed her by her hair and yanked her to her feet.

"Get up and go put some clothes on so we can leave."

"Oww, stop Gino! You're hurting me." She yelled trying to swarm out of my grip.

"Shut the fuck up before I start beating yo ass."

"Please stop, Gino… please doesn't hurt me I don't want to lose our baby…," she whispered while grabbing her stomach.

"What…? What did you just say?"

"I said I'm pregnant. I'm carrying your baby…, "I couldn't believe what she just told me…carrying my baby?

I let go of her hair, and let what she said soak in. This bitch just stood here and told me that she was carrying my baby, she was also fucking my brother on the regular, but she knew that baby was mine. This bitch must be crazy to tell me some shit like that. But who the father of the baby can't be determined until she has the baby so we could take a DNA test. It ain't like we can go off of looks.

"Alright, go put some clothes on so we can leave," I said in a calm matter.

"Why, where are we going?" she asked with fear in her eyes.

"I'm dropping you off at my Mama house. We're going to stay there for a couple days until I find us somewhere else to stay. Stop crying, everything gone be alright, you hear me?" she nodded her head yes. "Come here and give me a hug, I forgive you baby girl. I still love you and I always will." I whispered in her ear as she held on to me tight.

"I'm so sorry baby."

261

"I know, it's gone be okay. Now go get dressed so we can get up outta here, I'll wait out here for you," I kissed Zaria on the lips as I wiped her tears away.

She broke our embrace, gave me an appreciative smile, and proceeded to walk to the bedroom. But once her back was facing me, I slid the knife out of my right sleeve, grabbed her from behind, and slit her throat from ear to ear. She stumbled forward grabbing her neck, and then slowly turned to face me. She was unable to scream due to her trachea being cut in half. Blood was rushing through her fingers dripping on the clean white carpet, and her eyes were wide with shock. Her lips were moving but no words were coming out. She took one hand off her neck, and reached out to grab me but I took a quick step back. I didn't want to get any blood on me at all; the forensics these days could detect a speck of blood. The look of shock was replaced by anguish which cause a few tears to drop from my eyes.

Zaria finally dropped to her knees, and then face down in the stained carpet. Her lifeless body laid there still as a dark night. I just slit the throat of the woman I've been loving since I first experienced what love was. She was supposed to be my other half, my future wife, the future mother of my child, my confidant, my everything. I killed my everything and now she was gone forever. I couldn't live with the fact she betrayed me the way she did. My heart wouldn't forgive her. My mind wanted to…but my heart overpowered it.

I bent down and wiped the blood off the knife with the towel wrapped around her body, then stuck it in my jacket pocket. I looked at Zaria one last time.

"I'm sorry baby," I whispered as tears continued to fall. "I'll always love you….," I wiped away the tears with my sleeve. "…always."

Chapter Twenty-Eight

Mitch

I pulled up to the weight house on Park grove in my Buick Century, which was the car I always, drove when it was time to transport. I just got off the phone with Gino and he told me he was already there with Smurf waiting on me to come get them bricks. I'm glad I was able to trick Gino into thinking I was a solid nigga. I needed him to trust me, and after the incident at the mall, he just knew he had a real nigga on his team. But once I could get him and Slime to agree to meet with each other to squash the beef, I'll set both of them up. If I could get them to meet each other, Agent Graham agreed to help me plant kilos of heroin in their cars. So for now I had to accommodate Gino until my plan came to fruition.

I got outta my car and headed to the porch of the untidy weight house. I knocked lightly, and Smurf answered the door immediately.

"What's good my nigga?" Smurf greeted me with affection.

"What's the word, Smurf? How you been living?" I asked when I stepped into the house.

"I'm tryna get this guap my dude," I heard you put on a performance with them pistols the other day," he joked.

"Nawl man, I just did what I do best," I humbly responded. I knew Gino was go brag about me, and that let me know my mission was halfway completed.

"Yeah, I hear you my nigga. Gino happy you on the team so never take advantage of that," he warned me.

"Trust me I won't, I'm too loyal."

"I hope so. That nigga Gino in the basement, follow me," I followed Smurf through the kitchen, and down the creaking stairs.

When I got to the bottom of the stairs I followed him as he went left, then all of a sudden somebody grabbed me from behind! I tried to get loose but that didn't help because Smurf had his gun pressed against my forehead!

"Nigga if you make one move its over for you," Smurf told me through clenched teeth. The nigga behind me let me go, but continued to stand behind me so I couldn't see who it was.

"Man what the fuck is going on?" I asked scared to death!

"We ain't into talking that much," said the voice behind me, and that let me know it wasn't Gino. But where the fuck was Gino?

"Listen, I don't know what the fuck going on, but once Gino find out about this, y'all niggaz go regret it!" I said trying to show some type of toughness, but I was beginning to panic!

"That's some funny shit right there! Gino a real nigga, he would never ride for a snitch like you!" spat the voice behind me, and I could feel the chill in my bones when I heard the word snitch. I knew it was all over.

"Tell Lo-Lo Gino said save him a bed."

BLAH! BLAH! BLAH!

Chapter Twenty-Nine

Ace

"Why the fuck isn't Mitch answering his phone?" I looked over and asked Mel.

I was driving my Range Rover up Gratiot on my way to the Good life Lounge downtown. I had been trying to call Mitch all the day and he hasn't answered his phone once. He probably was mad at me because I had been slacking on handling business, but I been stressing lately. I have been going through a lot of shit for the past month so I deserved to take a break.

"I don't know nigga, I ain't his babysitter! He most likely laid up with a bitch somewhere, you know he love tricking!" joked Mel.

"That may be true, but it's unusual for that nigga to not answer his phone. After we leave the club we go check on Mack and Grey to see if he over there. But right now we bout to hit up this club, and enjoy our self," I stated as I stopped at a red light, pulled an already rolled blunt outta the console, and put fire to it.

The encounter I had with Gino earlier was still fresh on my mind, and him leaving me standing in the rain hurt me in the worst way. I wasn't surprised that he found out about Zaria and my secret relationship, I knew one day the truth would come to the light. But I was shocked that he found out about me telling Lucky that he robbed and killed Mook!

I was hurt without a doubt because Gino was my brother, but I wanted him dead so I could continue to run my enterprise by my lonesome! Getting rid of Gino would've put me in the position to make millions, and pay my workers the very minimum. And then the icing on the cake was I could have Zaria all to myself! I expected him to do something to me at the cemetery, but to my surprise he just walked away which had me wondering what he have planned. I knew for a fact he probably cut Zaria off so I had been trying to call her, but she wasn't answering her phone either. Oh well, I was out to have a good time tonight, and put all my worries to the side, and that's what I planned to do.

I pulled up to the club, and tossed my keys to the valet then proceeded towards the entrance. I greeted the bouncer that I was familiar with, then slid him two franklins even though I left my gun under the driver's seat. The club was packed as usual, and the music was pounding through "the state of the art speakers.

"I'm taking one of these to the telly tonight! Or maybe even two!" Mel yelled over the music

"That's the goal my nigga! Let's grab us a table so we can scope out our prey!" I yelled back as I led the way to the VIP section.

Two hours later, and four empty bottles of Remy Martin VSOP later, I was wasted and barely coherent! I could hear my words slurring, my head was swaying from side to side, and my vision was blurry. But I was feeling good because sitting next to me was the sexiest bitch in the whole club! She was Puerto Rican, Italian, or something of that nature. Her name was Maria… I think, or was it Maria? I just wanted to slide in her guts and fall asleep!

"Sooo… what you got up for tonight, sexy?" I finally cut into her.

"I was hoping I could spend tonight with you, papi," she replied while rubbing my inner thigh.

That was all I needed to hear! I glanced over at Mel, and he was in his zone. He was sitting between two dark young dimes with his arms draped around both of their necks. He said he was leaving with two hoes, I guess he was putting the finishing touches on his game.

"Aye Mel," I yelled across the table.

"What's good bro?" he immediately responded.

"Listen bro, me and shorty about to get up on a room, what you bout to do?" I asked while wrapping my arms around my lady.

"I'm straight bro, I'm go post up for a little while longer, and then these ladies will be my designated drivers! Right ladies?" Mel asked them, and they giggled while shaking their head yes.

I stood to my feet and damn near fell back down, and that caused Mel to burst out laughing! I made sure I could stand up before I made an attempt at walking, and my companion for the night wrapped her arm around my waist and helped me. I saluted my nigga Mel before I left the club with my designated driver holding me up. After valet reemerged with my truck, I told her to drive us to a hotel of her choice, then I leaned my seat all the way back and closed my eyes to hopefully stop the city from spinning.

Thirty minutes later instead of pulling up to a hotel, we pulled into the driveway of a nice sized house that was located in a suburban neighborhood. While she was driving I fucked around and dozed off, and now I don't have a clue where we were. I put the seat in the upright position as she pulled my truck into a garage.

"Where the fuck we at? This ain't a hotel!" I said, my head still slightly spinning.

"We are going to a room silly, my room! Why spend money and have a time limit, when we could just come here and not worry about anything. I don't want any distractions," she leaned over and kissed me on the lips. Are you cool with that," she asked.

"Yeah, that's cool with me. Anybody else live here with you?"

"Yup, my sister does but she over her boyfriend house for the night. So it's just me and you tonight, daddy," she moaned as she tongue kissed me, and massaged my dick through my pants!

"You keep this up we ain't go make it in the house!" I half joked. She chuckled lightly, and shut off the engine.

We both got outta the truck and made our way to a door that connected the garage to the house. I staggered up a few steps, and walked through the door that led to the kitchen. She cut on a light switch in the kitchen, a red light came on and I was caught completely off guard at the scene! Everything in the kitchen was red, it wasn't another color in sight! It was as if the color caused my head to spin faster!

"DAMN! What's up with all this red?" I asked, trying to adjust to the bright solid color.

"I decorated my whole house red, that's my favorite color!" she noticed the color draining from my face.

"I'm straight…, "I leaned against the counter to get my balance.

"Let's just get to yo room before I fall on my face."

I followed her through the house and realized and wasn't joking, this bitch decorated her whole house red! She had to be a little crazy or something to go through with an idea like that. Who decorated their whole fucking house the same color?

271

After climbing the stairs, we walked to the end of the hallway, and she opened the door leading to her bedroom. Without warning she turned around, grabbed my face, and stuck her tongue down my throat. I fondled her curvy body as we back peddled to her king size bed where we flopped down on, still entangled in each other arms. She straddled me and snatches off my t-shirt and tossed it to the floor. Next, she pulled her skin-tight dress over her head, and tossed it to the floor too. She wasn't wearing a bra but her ample titties still stood firm, and to my surprise she wasn't wearing panties either! My dick was already hard in my pants, and I didn't want to wait any longer. I begin to unbuckle my belt then all of a sudden she got up from the bed.

"What are you doing?" I asked in desperation.

"Calm down papi," she instructed me while walking towards the bathroom that was connected to her room. "I need to freshen this pussy up for you, it'll only be a couple minutes so be ready when I return," then she disappeared into the bathroom, closing the door behind her.

I stood up and quickly took off my pants and boxers after kicking off my Mauri gym shoes. I hastily got under the sheets and begin to stroke myself, anticipating the return of whatever her name was. She was back a few minutes later, and she slithered to the bed with the precision of a snake moving in on its prey. She snatched the sheets off me and tossed them to the floor with the pile of clothes. She begins kissing my whole body starting at my feet, and gently working her way up to my

272

manhood. Waiting for the inevitable to happen, I tilted my head back and closed my eyes.

Instead of feeling a warm sensation of her mouth, I felt cold metal touch the shaft of my dick. Before I could look and see what it was I felt the worst pain I ever felt in my whole life! My breath was caught up in my throat so I was unable to scream! I looked down to see my dick detached from my body, and then I finally found my voice.

"Aaagghhh! Biiittttccchhhh!" I wailed as tears of pain streamed down my face.

Blood was pouring out of where my dick used to be, and I was in shock! My eyes darted to the bitch, which name I still didn't know, and she was now standing at the foot of the bed with a smirk on her face and my penis in her left hand! I almost fainted but realized I couldn't lose consciousness. What the fuck was going on? The blood was hot and sticky as it covered my pelvic bone, and thighs.

"Why…Why…?" was all I could say as I tried my hardest to control my breathing.

"Because you won't need it anymore," said a deep voice that was unseen.

I looked over at the bathroom door and could see a shadow standing there. I squinted my eyes to try to make out the towering silhouette, but I couldn't. I attempted to get up but was in too much pain move.

"Ain't no sense in getting up now, just relax," said the shadow.

"Who is that man? I need to get to the hospital!" I yelled. I could feel my body become weak.

"Oh, you don't know who I am?" said the shadow as he slowly made his way to the bed. "Surprise, surprise my nigga," said Slime as he stood smiling down at me.

My eyes became wide with terror once I seen that my worst nightmare was standing over me. And it all made sense, this bitch set me up! It was finally over for me now. My gun was in the truck, and I was laying naked and dickless! I couldn't believe I was still conscious! The pain was excruciating and I couldn't take it much longer.

"Do what yo go do muthafucka! I ain't going out like a bitch, so kill me and get it over with."

"Well, well, well, aren't you a tough little cookie," said Slime clearly amused. "Why are you so eager to die now?" he asked as he pulled a Glock .40 from his pocket.

"I ain't got any reason to live now...my dick gone!" I replied with a sinister laugh, and Slime laughed too.

He walked over to the still naked bitch that set him up, and kissed her on the cheek. He handed the gun to her, and then sat in a chair in the far corner of the room.

"You got any last wishes my nigga? Any messages you want me to deliver," Slime offered.

"Yeah…," I had to think for a second before I continued. "Tell my Mama I'm sorry for putting her through so much pain, and I love her. And…," tears begin to flow as I thought about Gino. "Tell Gino… I'm sorry for everything… and I'll make it up to him in another life."

"Is that all?"

"Nawl… tell him to bury me next to Autumn. I know if they don't he'll never visit my grave."

"Aight, I got yo lil bro. I love you with all my heart Ace, and I'll see you when my time is up. Hopefully by that time you'll forgive me," Slime looked at the female, and nodded his head slightly. She raised the gun and begins to empty the whole clip in my numb body.

Chapter Thirty

Gino

It's been a little over a week since the police found Ace's naked body on the porch of the house we grew up in on Wade street. He was shot thirty-two times in the torso, and they found his own dick shoved down his throat! I was asking myself why they picked the house we grew up in to dump his body, and then I realized how symbolic the message was. They dumped him there to basically say never forget where you came from.

The funeral was yesterday, and I wasn't going attend it but I had to be there for my Mama. It hurt like hell to see my little brother lying in a casket at such a young age, but with all the pain flowing through my heart I still found it hard to cry. I buried my little sister, then my little brother mere weeks apart. And I did as Ace desired, I buried him right next to Autumn. May God bless both their souls?

My Mama was devastated to the point where I suggested that she move to Lansing with her sister Tamia. She of course refused at first, but decided to move with her until she healed from her broken heart. I didn't want to tell her, but I didn't think broken hearts healed. I couldn't imagine losing two of my children in the same month, I would probably go insane. I was just happy she was outta Detroit because I didn't want her to live here once I moved to Tulsa, Oklahoma tomorrow morning.

Destiny and I were ready to leave Michigan behind, take all the money I saved up, and start a new life. It wasn't anything left for me in Detroit but bad memories! The beef between me and the red Mafiya was over, but the Mexican mafia was still looking for me. Those bitches gone have to find me!

They found Zaria's body the same night I killed her, and I was of course a suspect. Homicide detectives stopped by my Mama house that following day looking for me for questioning. Once my Mama called me, I had Destiny take me down to the Homicide Headquarters. After an hour of questioning, I was allowed to leave. I told them I had been broke up with her when I found out she was using drugs, and I used Destiny as my alibi on my whereabouts.

Right after I left them, I got the call from Murda letting me know that Mitch will never be seen again. I dropped Destiny off at home and met him and Smurf at Chandler Park. They told me they took his body to a vacant warehouse and burned his body in a huge furnace. I told them that I was leaving the state and didn't plan on coming back. They were sad that I was leaving, but was happy that I was leaving behind my connect, and all the spots I had. I still had ten kilo's of heroin unsold so I gave each of them five apiece. I put my niggaz in a position to continue to get money while I start my new life that was my gift to them for remaining loyal.

I thought back to when we had the meeting after Autumn's funeral, and I asked myself who was the flaw in our circle. And now it was only three of us standing at the end that remained real. Life had a funny way of showing you who's really there for you, and it turns out it was two niggaz I met in prison.

Destiny was still down for me, and she was the happiest woman in the world! She couldn't wait until we left the state in the morning, and I felt the same way. The money I made over the past four months was more than I ever dreamed about having! I was on my way to Oklahoma with 9.3 million in cash! I knew I couldn't take it with me on the plane, so I hired a U-Haul driver to transport the money to our new house. I stuffed the money inside a couple of old couches, and sewed it back up. I put a bunch of frivolous furniture and appliance in the back of the truck too, so the couches wouldn't draw attention if the driver was pulled over. The driver started its journey earlier today so it should be waiting on us when we arrived.

Right now I was laid up with my future wife watching the news. It was around 5'O'clock at night and I didn't have any plans to leave the house. That was until I got a dreadful text message from Nadia:

GINO, I'M PREGNANT! PLEASE CALL ME!!

If it wasn't one thing it was another! I haven't seen or talked to Nadia since the day I broke it off with her, and she didn't take the break-up very well! Every single day she blew up my phone, sent me text messages, and left voicemails. I never did answer her calls so I know she was desperate enough to pull the pregnant move on me. Rather I wanted to or not, I had to go see her to clarify if she was pregnant or not. If she was in fact pregnant, then that would put a strain on my relationship with Destiny.

Destiny and I were lying in bed together watching some movie I wasn't even paying attention to. She had her head resting on my chest while rubbing my stomach.

"Aye baby," I whispered in her ear.

"Huh…?" she replied, raising her head up to look me in the eyes.

"You know I love you to death, right?"

"Yes, I know. I love you too baby, but what's on your mind?" she asked me.

"I just wanted to let you know before we take this big step tomorrow. Ain't no looking back now, we in it for the long haul" I planted a wet kiss on her lips.

"You damn right we in it for the long haul! I'm with you baby, I got your back through thick and thin. And I mean that with all of my heart, Gino," I could tell she meant every word by looking in her eyes. I had a winner on my team, and now it seemed like my life was finally coming together even after all the people I lost in the process.

"Did you talk to the Realtor in Tulsa today?" I asked switching the subject to make sure business was taken care of at our new home.

"Yes I did. According to him the house is already ready for us to move in. He'll be waiting on our arrival tomorrow."

"Good. What about the U-Haul driver? Do you have his cell phone number?" I was concerned about the millions he was transporting even though he didn't know that all that money was hidden in the couches.

"Yes I do baby. I'll call him in a couple hours to check his location, and make sure everything in on schedule. Don't worry baby, I got everything under control. Our transition to our new life will be smooth," she assured.

"I love that you on your job, it's just the hustler in me that have to make sure everything is in order," I told her as I got up from the bed, and grabbed my pants from off the chair.

"Where do you think you going?"

"I need to handle some business real quick before we leave."

"How long are you going to be gone?" she asked with an attitude.

"Don't trip boo; I'll be back in a couple hours at the least. You acting like I'm not coming back or something," I walked back to the bed once I was fully dressed, and leaned down to kiss her.

"You better come back!" she replied.

"Don't worry I will, aight?"

"Aight. Just don't have me waiting up all night."

"I won't."

"You promise?"

"Yeah, I promise," I said kissing her again.

"I love you."

"I love you too," I slapped her on the ass, and walked outta the room.

I had left the room, but turned back around when something came to me. I took a step back and stuck my head through the door.

"Oh yeah, I got a surprise for you when I get back," I told Destiny.

"Whaaaat…? What is it?" she asked with excitement.

"If I told you it wouldn't be a surprise!" I smiled at her anxious facial expression, and then ran outta the house.

Chapter Thirty-One

Gino

I arrived at Nadia's apartment thirty minutes later in my Aston Martin. I decided to store the Aston Martin in the garage at the house I bought for Destiny, that way I'll have a nice home and car at my disposal whenever I visited Detroit.

It was still early so the sun was shining bright and the heat was overwhelming. I activated the alarm once I exited the expensive car, and begin to speed walk up to the building. Instead of using the elevator I took the stairs up to the third floor. I rang the doorbell several times before she finally answered it.

Her overall appearance was disgruntled, and rugged as if she hasn't left her apartment in weeks. I looked at her and shook my head in disgust. She stepped forward and tried to put her arms around me, but I gently declined by sticking my arms out to stop her. Her eyes begin to get watery, and I could see the pain of rejection written all over her face.

"I didn't come over here to comfort you, Nadia. I came to see if you're really pregnant or not," I said in a stern voice, and her eyes diverted to her feet as she tried to avoid eye contact.

She walked away from the door, and took a seat on the sofa, leaving me still standing at the door. I stepped into the apartment and closed the door behind me. As I slowly walked towards Nadia, the stench of her body odor burned the hairs in my nostrils! This girl hasn't been washing her ass? I decided not to say anything about the smell, it wasn't my problem.

"Listen Nadia, I'm not going to be here long so go get the test- better yet, I want you to take a new test while I'm here," I requested while my hand was covering my nose.

'Oh, so you don't believe me, Gino? You think I would lie to you about something like this?" she asked with a hint of distress seething out of her pores.

"I'm not saying I don't believe you, I just need to make sure-"

"What? Make sure I'm not trying to play you for your money? I don't give a fuck about your money; all I ever wanted was you! And why the fuck are you holding your nose!?! She yelled, and I was ready to leave already.

"I don't have time for this shit, Nadia," I said calmly. "I'll tell you what, since you want to procrastinate this whole ordeal, I'll see you in a couple months," I announced and then turned to leave.

"What do you mean a couple months?" I turned back around to face her, and felt a slight bit of remorse once I noticed the tears pouring down her face.

"Please don't leave me, Gino! Can't you see I can't function without you?" Nadia screamed.

"Tomorrow I'm leaving the state rather you like it or not. I'm starting a new life with a new beginning. So after I get settled in I'll come back to check on you. If you are pregnant when I come back, I'll keep in contact until the baby is born. We'll get a DNA test to prove if I'm the father or not. That is the plan to eliminate all the games-"

"Fuck you nigga! You don't have to believe shit I say, but when that child support starts eating at them pockets, I don't want to hear your arrogant ass crying!"

"Bitch, I don't give a fuck about no child support! My money long enough to pay every nigga in Detroit child support! What the fuck is you talking bout you stanking ass bitch! Like I said, in the morning me and my future wife leaving the state flying first class! You better pray you pregnant with my seed, that'll be a privilege for yo tired ass!" I lost

284

my cool, and I could tell that I cut her deep when I mention my future wifey.

"So it was another bitch, huh? I was just your play thing, huh? That's what I was to you, Gino?" she asked.

I didn't even respond I just walked towards the door; I didn't have time for this shit.

"So you just go leave without answering me? Answer me damnit!" she yelled as she sprinted to the door and grabbed me. She spun me around and I could see the hatred in her heart that she had for me.

"Nadia… let me go," I calmly stated.

"You know what Gino," she released her grasp from my arm, and opened the front door. 'You can leave, I don't need you anyway boo, boo. You can't do anything for me, especially after the feds arrest your ass."

"What the fuck you just say?" Nadia crossed her arms across her chest, and a smirk appeared on her face.

"All that shit you talking about moving with your future Wifey, and all the money you got won't mean shit when you back in prison praying somebody write you a letter or visit you. I told the fed who you were, and what you do for a living. I told yo ass if I couldn't have you no one would!" she said with so much assurance that I believed every word she said. I stood there staring at her dumbfounded.

"What? You ain't got nothing to say now?" she taunted.

"Nadia... Please tell me you just running yo mouth. Please tell me what you just said was all talk," I pleaded

"No boo boo, what I just said was the truth. I called them, told them that you sell dope, and now they are investigating you right now, big money." Next thing I knew I had Nadia stretched out on the couch with my hands wrapped around her neck so tight that my veins were bulging on the back of them!

"Bitch is you crazy! You called the fucking feds on me! Do you know that I will kill you!?!" I screamed, I wanted so bad to end her life, and it took everything in my power to pry my hands loose.

I stood up and looked down at her with my chest heaving up and down from the adrenaline pumping in my heart. Nadia had fear written all over her face, and her body was trembling as she rubbed her neck.

"I'm sorry.... Gino! Please don't hurt me, I just didn't want to lose you! I'm soooorrryyy....," she begged for forgiveness, but I didn't care if God himself came to me and told me to forgive her, it wouldn't happen!

I wanted to kill her, but it wouldn't be a smart thing to do. I didn't know if the feds were watching me right now or not. Instead of fucking her up, I shook my head in disbelief and stormed outta the apartment. I could hear Nadia screaming at the top of her lungs for me to come back, but I kept it moving. I took the stairs again and made it outside quicker than normal. As I was walking towards my car, Nadia came running out of the building.

"Gino, I will fucking shoot you if you don't stop!" she shot once in the air, and I stopped in my tracks. "Come here, Gino!" she demanded.

I slowly turned around to see Nadia holding a Glock .9 millimeter with both hands, aiming right at me. This bitch done lost her muthafucking mind!

"Nadia put that gun down before somebody see you and call the police," I said in a calm voice as I slowly eased towards her.

"No! I'm not putting shit down! Stop walking!" she yelled and I froze where I stood.

"You need to calm down, and be smart. Put the gun down and go back into the building before something stupid happen."

"I don't care anymore! I don't care about life, school, money, I don't care about nothing but you! I can't let you leave me, Gino."

'Nadia I'm leaving rather you like it or not. So… if yo go shoot me then shoot me, because-"

BLAH! BLAH!

"OH, MY, GOD! WHAT DID I DO!?! WHAT DID I DO!?!" I could hear Nadia screams as she eased her way to me and dropping the gun in the process.

Blood was pouring from my chest. I dropped to my knees, and then face down on the scorching concrete. My chest felt like it collapsed and it was becoming hard to breath. Nadia kneeled down over me and cried until a crowd started to form around me. I could tell that she didn't really want to shoot me; she just didn't want to live without me. Why couldn't I see that?

I tried to tell her that I still loved her, but no words came out, I was too busy trying to breath. My lips were moving, and my blood was spilling outta my mouth. A lot of commotion was going on around me, and I saw that Nadia had zoned out in her own thoughts. She didn't even notice the police had arrived until an officer took her by the arm.

"Excuse me ma'am, I need you to get face down on the ground, and place your hands behind your head," ordered the white male officer.

"You need to get him to the hospital," I heard her beg the officer.

"We understand that lady, but you need to do as I said first," he replied, and I was now fading in and out of consciousness.

I came to long enough to see Nadia' following the police orders and lying face down not knowing what her future held.

"I'm sorry Gino. I will always love you, baby," she whispered to me, and then I faded into darkness.

Epilogue:

Destiny

Just when Destiny thought her life was near perfect the unthinkable happens, she loses the love of her life. Her dreams of moving out of state and settling down with Gino came to an abrupt halt. Her dreams were shattered in the blink of an eye, and the only thing that soothes some of her heartache is knowing that the life growing inside of her stomach will be a piece of him still on earth.

"Will everybody give a round of applause to the UNITY CHURCH OF GOD IN CHRIST choir," requested Pastor Thomas as everybody greeted the youthful singers.

Destiny was sitting on the first pew holding Gino's mother hand while Gino was laying peacefully in his expensive Gucci suit, and twenty thousand dollar marble casket. Destiny avoided looking directly at his inflated body; it only led to her shedding more tears. And as of lately, all she did was cry.

She cried for Gino dying so young. She cried for her unborn child, knowing that her child will never know who its father was. She cried for his mother who lost all three of her children in a two month time frame, and Destiny knew she had to be devastated. Finally she cried for her future, not really knowing if she'll ever recover from her strife.

290

If only Gino would've stayed at home with her he would've still been alive. She was hurt but happy that he left behind memories that she would cherish forever. He left behind enough knowledge to understand life as a whole, and she would apply all that knowledge to live a prosperous life for her unborn child. And not to mention he left behind 9.3 million dollars in cash!

When Destiny found out that Gino had been murdered by some deranged bitch, she called the driver of the U-Haul truck that was taking the money to Tulsa, and instructed him to come back to Detroit.

Destiny gave Gino's mother 4 million dollars, and stashed the rest. The house that he bought her in Farmington Hills was in her name, so a roof over her head wasn't an issue. She was defiantly financially stable for years to come, and she was still working on getting her real estate license. Gino would be so proud of her.

The only thing that was eating at her brain was, not knowing what the surprise was that Gino had for her before he got killed. But she soon found out the day she picked up his Aston Martin from the police impound the following week. Once she got the car back she found an engagement ring in the glove compartment, and broke down in tears staring at the eight carat diamond ring resting in the small black velvet box. Gino had planned to ask her to marry him; on top of that she was pregnant with his baby. But they never got the chance to tell each other their surprises. Life was a dirty game.

The choir harmonizing broke destiny's trance, she still couldn't believe she was attending the father of her first and possible only child funeral. She still had so much to tell him, and so many secrets to come clean about. She had every intention on telling Gino her secrets, but the opportunity never presented itself. But now he would never know and she felt she wasn't all the way loyal to him by holding these secrets.

Dark secrets...

Prologue:

Lil Gee

"It's about time you decided to join the family, Lil Gee. You know this where you belong anyway," said Seven.

"Yeah, I already know my nigga. I just wanted to make sure this is where I wanted to be," Lil Gee replied as he hit the OG Kush blunt.

Lil Gee was parked outside of Seven's grandma house in his newly bought 2018 Mercedes Benz his moms purchased for him on his recently passed birthday. Any 14 year old would be exhilarated to be driving a Benz at a young age, but Lil Gee was different. His family had plenty of money so it meant nothing to him. From what he was told, his father was the reason he was living a comfortable life. In fact, he was named after his father: Gerald Giovanni Irby III. He heard his father was a killer, and a major drug dealer, and he left his moms with millions when he was murdered by some crazy bitch.

It was only so much Lil Gee did know about his father, but that didn't stop him from idolizing his father who he never got to meet. From what his mother told him, his father never knew his mom was pregnant before he was killed. But Lil Gee planned to represent his pops absence at all cost.

Today Lil Gee was joining the biggest blood set in the country: The Red Mafiya. Lil Gee vowed people will never forget about him when he dies. Just like people still respected his father, he wanted the same respect.

Coming Soon

LOVE THY ENEMIES II

Blood B4 Dishonor

BIO

H.B. SALLE was born on the Eastside of Detroit. LOVE THY ENEMIES is his debut urban Novel. He enjoys writing novels, music and poetry daily and is currently putting the finishing touches on LOVE THY ENEMIES II. You can check him out on Facebook